CAM

WOUNDED HEROES #2

AVA MANELLO

Jeanette
Hope you enjoy
Cam mm lae
Ava
Manello x

Cam by Ava Manello

© 2018, Ava Manello

KBK Publishing

ISBN: 978-0-9932436-2-2

Cover Designer: Francessca Wingfield

This book is dedicated to my Mum, Sue Wells. The strongest, most loved person you could ever hope to meet. So many people called her friend, but I was lucky enough to be her daughter. She passed away whilst I was writing this book. There isn't a day goes by that I don't miss her and wish she was here. She was a huge supporter of my writing, and in life was always there when I needed her. If I can be a fraction of the woman that she was, then I will have lived my life well.

To the memory of the 'Wonder of Sue'

PROLOGUE

Cam

The room is dimly lit, and I'm almost choking on the smoke from Jerry's fat cigar. It looks like it's more for show as I rarely see him inhaling. The lack of light serves to make the room look better than it is. Shabby chic is an improvement on what I see when I look too closely into the shadows. Jerry may think he's the big man, but I see through the façade. He's a wannabe, a guy who thinks he's a player, surrounding himself with some tattooed muscle to make him look important. If it wasn't for his family connections he'd be a nobody, but his uncle runs the local area and puts up with him for his mother's sake.

His almost non-existent neck is encased in gaudy, thick gold chains whilst his chubby fingers sport large gold rings that barely fit. With his dinner suit and a dark shirt that strains across his ample belly I'm reminded of a bad seventies porn movie. The stubble on his triple chin is too long to be trendy and too short to be worthy of being called a beard. It's scruffy and unattractive. His fat bushy eyebrows over-shadow narrow beady eyes. A dark fedora balances atop his greasy sable hair, a triple black gingham ribbon loosely wrapped around the base.

The girl hovering behind his chair is worth a second glance or three. She's stunning, or she would be if she didn't look so numb. She has long ash blonde hair that flows gracefully over her shoulders. I can't quite make out her eyes in this light, they could be grey I guess, but there's no spark in them. Her slender figure is encased in a sheer white robe that reveals simple white underwear.

She exudes class and innocence, a total contrast to Jerry. A long fine gold chain attached to a leather cuff binds her fore-arm, the other end secured around Jerry's wrist. After a few hands have been dealt he yanks on the chain pulling her closer. Drawing her face down to his he runs his tongue along her cheek before whispering obscenities too loudly in her ear. He wants the rest of us in the room to hear him. She's no more than an accessory to him, just like the ostenta-tious but gauche jewelry he's adorned himself with. She's a good actress, but I don't miss the shiver of disgust every time his flesh comes into contact with hers. What the hell is she doing here?

I'm beginning to regret being drawn into the card game, but it was a way of relieving the boredom of the bike ride back home. Normally I love being out on the bike, but after our recent action in Severed everything feels like an anti-climax. I've won a few hands and lost a few. Jerry's no match for me. All those nights in Afghanistan helped me hone my poker skills. I'm not bragging when I say I'm good,

good enough to go professional if I wanted. Jerry is cocky, but his arrogance is going to cost him. I've lulled him into a false sense of security and he's starting to gamble heavily now. I've made enough deliberate mistakes to convince him I'm an amateur. I'm going to enjoy bringing the arrogant shit down.

I hold back a growl as he once again yanks the girl to him, this time pawing at her breasts which are barely contained in the flimsy clothing he has her wearing. "Do you like my new toy?" he asks the table.

There are four of us playing poker tonight. It's an illegal game as Jerry is keeping the buy-in, it's not being returned to the winner. The other two are tired looking businessmen who seem to be a little too in awe of Jerry. I'm guessing it's a scam he runs instead of a more traditional protection racket. They come play and walk away empty handed. I can see that they're deliberately playing bad hands.

Jerry gestures to the girl, telling us that she's a new arrival to his 'stable' that he's looking forward to breaking in after the game. Right now, I want to punch the arrogant prick in the throat. "If you're interested I'll offer you a good price for her when I'm finished" he gloats. Fuck me. The guys a pimp as well as an arsehole. He introduces her as Sahara, an unusual name I'm sure he's made up to suit his little fantasy. Meanwhile the expression has left her face altogether, the more he talks, the more withdrawn she becomes.

We play a few more games, some I win, some I lose. The more I lose the more Jerry drinks, his confidence and arrogance increasing with each shot of whisky. He's playing right into my hands.

Finally, I spot my opportunity. The stupid fuck has no poker face and I can see the grin he tries to hide when he's dealt the next hand. I deliberately grimace then try to disguise it when I look at my hand, and he falls for it. By now we're about evenly matched in money on the table. He places the last of his money down, he's all in.

I take my opportunity. "How about we make this a little more interesting?" I place my bike keys on the table. Jerry was enthralled with my bike when I arrived, although I'm pretty sure he's never ridden one, he's probably too heavy to be able to balance my Triumph although he might get away with a Harley. He looks at his hand again. He's so confident it's the winner that he makes a ridiculous bet. He offers the girl, his shiny new toy for the evening. I'm a better player than he realizes, I know I've got an unbeatable hand.

"How does that work?" I'm curious.

"I own her," he responds smugly. "You win, then you own her." He states it so simply. I have to resist the urge to smash his face in. His haughtiness is misplaced, his ignorant manner rubbing me up the wrong way.

It's time to show our hands, Jerry goes first, and his arrogant grin gets even bigger as he places his cards fanned out, face up on the table. One by one a straight flush of hearts appears, 5,6,7,8 and 9.

His grin stays there, right until I place my last card down. The ace of spades completing my Royal Flush, then it changes to a look of anger.

He pulls Sahara to him, yanking the gold chain violently. "You're mine," he practically spits into her face. "I'm not giving up what's mine."

"A bet's a bet, I'd like to take my winnings now." I stand from the table, pocketing the cash, my voice firm but polite. Casually I ease back my jacket showing the gun I have holstered on my side. His bodyguards are too slow to respond, I've already placed the barrel of the gun against his sweating forehead before they've had a chance to draw their weapons. With my free hand I motion to Sahara to release herself from the cuff. She seems to take forever. When she's done I toss her the leather jacket from the back of my chair.

"We'll be leaving now. I'd be grateful if you'd escort me out, Jerry. It's only polite after all." With my gun still aimed at him I gesture to Jerry to rise from his seat. His face is a mask of fury, but he does as he's told.

Within moments we're out back of the building where I've parked my bike. With one hand aiming the gun at Jerry I start the bike with the other. Sahara looks reluctant to climb on behind me until I tell her it's her only option if she doesn't want to be left behind. That gets a reaction. She's got goosebumps in the cool night air, and I'm reluctant to take her on the bike considering the lack of clothing she has on. She's still carrying my jacket. I gesture for her to put it on, but she's taking too long. As I help her into it, swapping the gun from hand to hand gives Jerry a false sense of security and he tries to make a move on us. I'm too quick for him, firing a shot into the dust at his feet. He stalls his advance, all the while swearing and threatening us, promising he'll hunt us down and kill me. His goons still hover in the doorway of the building waiting for me to lower my gun, so they can take their chance.

Pulling my mobile from my shirt pocket I speed dial

Declan. This situation is out of control, and I'm going to need him to help me make peace with Jerry's uncle.

"Declan, you know when we said we'd be there for each other if needed? You meant it right?"

"Of course I did, Cam," Declan answers. "What's wrong?". He sounds concerned.

"Declan, I need you." No sooner have I spoken the words than one of the bodyguards fires a shot at us, he misses but it's a little too close for comfort. With the gun still in my left hand I'm left with no choice but to drop the phone, so I can throttle the bike and get us out of here.

1

Cam

I'm speeding away from the bar with no real idea of where to go next. Luckily most of my gear is already packed in the bike; there are only a few items of clothing and toiletries back at the hotel. I can afford to lose them, so I make the decision to not go back there. I'm pissed at having dropped my phone, but at least I can wipe it as soon as I reach a computer. The bastards won't be able to get into it and find anything.

I'm conscious that the girl is wearing barely any clothing; I need to get off the road and find somewhere safe for her. I heard the screech of tires not long after we sped off so I'm sure they're in pursuit and fairly close behind. It's a good job the bike is suitable for off road and I'm going to make use of that. As soon as I spy a dirt track that's too narrow for a car I turn into it. The surface is rutted and dry, making for uncomfortable riding, but right now escape is more important than comfort.

The night air has taken on a chill. I need to get the girl under cover somewhere; she must be frozen in that flimsy outfit. Her bare legs squeeze tightly against my hips, and I can feel how cold she is through my thin trousers. Whatever I do, I need to keep this bike upright; she's got no protection if we were to come off.

The grasp of her hands around my chest loosens. I reach back, pulling her arms tighter to me, one at a time. From the startled reaction, and the jolt of her body into a more rigid position when I touch her, I'm guessing the shock is wearing off and exhaustion has kicked in. Still, her hold tightens and that's just what I needed from her.

Who is this girl and where has she come from? She doesn't look like the kind of girl I'd expect to see around Jerry. There's something about her that makes me think she was out of place there. His normal harem looks like they've seen better days and are drugged to the eyeballs. Drugs would explain the numb expression on her face, leaving me with the additional worry of what she's got running through her system. Is she addicted to it already? I can probably source whatever she needs even though it would make it easier to track us if Jerry's determined.

I'm mentally calculating what I've got locked away in the bike against what we're going to need for the next few days, hoping I can at least get us through the night without having to go back on the main road. It's not going to be ideal, but it will have to do. Let's face it, I've faced far worse conditions over in Afghanistan, but something tells me the girl isn't used to roughing it. I curse myself for not being able to remember her name.

☙

We've been riding through the woods for around an hour when I see the flash of headlights from a road alongside us. I'm not a total stranger to the area yet can't quite get my bearings. The car appears to be traveling in the other direction. Once I'm certain it's out of range I head for the road. I'm relieved to see we've come out on a small highway that I'm familiar with. I'm pretty sure there's a motel not far from here and I'm hoping Jerry won't think of it. I'm guessing he'll strong arm his way into the hotel I was booked into then think I've left town altogether when he doesn't find me there. I know I shouldn't assume anything, but Jerry never was the sharpest tool in the box.

The acid light of the motel sign is a welcome sight in the dark night, especially when it states rooms available. I draw the bike to a halt in the darkest corner of the car park, away from prying eyes. The girl's grip tightens around me like a vice. From the way she's shaking it's more than just the cold, its shock manifesting itself.

"Wait here," I whisper to her. "In that outfit you're far too memorable. I'll be back out for you as soon as I can." She says nothing, drawing my jacket more tightly around her. She's contained herself a little and that numb mask of hers is covering her face again. She sits straight, her back rigid. "I promise you I'll be back," I offer. I'm relieved to see just a little of the tension leave her at these last words.

The campsite office smells of stale cooking grease and cigarettes. The young guy behind the counter is engrossed in a comic, the images of the superheroes remind me of my own childhood. I used to love getting a crisp new comic every month when I got my pocket money.

I pull myself from my nostalgia, swiftly booking a room. I manage to grab a few supplies of fresh bread, milk and bacon from a fridge on the wall while I'm there. The selection is limited, but it looks to be edible and right now that's all that matters.

I've asked for a room away from the road and checking the number on the over large keyring I'm pleased to see that I'm almost parked in front of it. The girl looks exhausted. I'll leave the bike where it is, get her settled, then come back and grab some gear.

I'm pleasantly surprised when I open the door. The set-up is basic, a double bed in the center of the room, a small hob, fridge and sink make up a kitchen area, and there's a sofa and coffee table in front of an open fireplace. I'm hoping the door off to the side is a shower.

The girl simply nods when I suggest she lie down and get some rest while I get my stuff.

Unpacking the minimum from my bike I return to the room to find her asleep. She's discarded my jacket and the lightweight wrap, sleeping in just her underwear. Her long blonde hair is strewn across the pillow. As she lays there on the bed, curled into herself and looking vulnerable, it's hard to believe that just hours ago she'd been someone's property, something to be gambled away on the turn of a card. Technically, I'm now her owner. That doesn't sit right with me.

Reassuring myself that she's soundly asleep and the doors are locked, I head for the shower. The warm water trickles from the grimy shower head, but it's better than nothing. Clean again I stand in front of the tiny mirror and shave away the day-old stubble, noticing the bags under my eyes. I feel like I've been living out of a suitcase or backpack forever.

I allow myself a moment to envy Declan. He's got roots now, a place he belongs. I'm also fairly sure he's got a surrogate family if he stays with Holly, the girl he met in Severed.

I've been away from home for so long I've forgotten what it feels like. My parents were pleased to see me when I left the Army and went back to Perth of course, but I'm not a teenager anymore. I need my own space, my own place.

I'd kill for a drink right now, but it wouldn't be wise. I need to keep my wits about me. I settle on the sofa, my eyes on the door, strong black coffee on the table and take first watch.

My job is to protect her... from the hell that I've unleashed.

2

Cam

*S*unlight filters through the too thin curtains, alerting me to the new day. Shit! I must have fallen asleep when I should have been keeping watch. Glancing quickly over to the bed I'm startled to see it empty. The sound of running water from the bathroom gives me some small comfort. The girl must be in the shower. I struggle to recall her name from last night, I was too focused on the poker game to have taken it in, but I do recall it sounding exotic.

Sasha, Sarah... no wait, Sahara, that's it. After the desert, I remember thinking at the time that it was an unusual name.

Walking over to my bag I retrieve a spare pair of boxers, jeans and a t-shirt, remembering to add in a belt to hold the jeans up. They're all going to be too big for her, but at least they'll be warm, clean and dry. I place them on the floor in front of the bathroom door, knocking gently to alert her to my presence. There's no response, the shower probably drowning me out.

I add cold water to the kettle from the sink in the kitchen realizing too late, when I hear a yelp from the bathroom, that I shouldn't run the water while the shower's on. Oops. Declan did the same thing to me when I stayed here once before. Setting the kettle to boil I start to make us both a drink, stopping when I discover I don't even know how she takes her coffee.

I'll just have to wait for her to finish.

A few minutes later the bathroom door creaks open slowly, but not fully. Being the gentleman that I am I turn my back, telling her that there are clean clothes on the floor, and she should feel free to use my toothbrush and toothpaste until we can get her one of her own. The door is about to shut tight again when I remember I didn't ask her how she takes her coffee. Doh. For someone who normally lives his life with military precision I seem to be making a mess of things here in civvy street.

"How do you like your coffee?" I quickly ask.

"Black, no sugar." Her reply is so softly spoken I strain to hear it. "Thank you," she adds, just before the door clicks closed again.

The motel may be rundown, but the coffee is a good quality for an instant brand and I savor it. I've almost finished my first cup when Sahara emerges from the bathroom. Even in clothes that are too large for her she looks stunning. She also looks fragile. My protective instinct kicks into overdrive. I don't know what her story is, but I do know that I'm not going to let anything bad happen to her again.

Moving slowly across the room she reminds me of a startled animal, her steps are cautious and deliberate. It only takes her a few moments to reach me yet the entire time she was alert to her surroundings, almost as if she was looking for an escape route. I really am slow this morning. I know that I mean her no harm, but what evidence does she have of that, other than me running off with her last night.

"It's okay, Sahara." I try and keep my voice gentle, calming, just like I would if I was on the farm working with a frightened colt. "I'm not going to hurt you."

Her grey eyes are full of suspicion when she looks at me. I honestly can't blame her. My mind doesn't even want to think about what she's suffered whilst being around Jerry and his cronies.

I motion to the sofa where I slept last night, bringing the coffee cups with me. She sits at one end, straight backed and alert. I choose the seat at the opposite end, sinking back into the comfortable cushions, yet allowing her as much space as I can. She almost groans when she takes the first sip of coffee. The sound is erotic, and I feel my cock twitch. I can't think of her in that way, so I try and replace the images in my head with pictures of the comic book heroes from my childhood. That helps.

"Who are you?" she asks hesitantly. "What are you going to do with me?" There's no fear in her voice, just a resigned acceptance which is worse.

"I'm Cam," I begin. "Its short for Cameron, but that's my Sunday name." I laugh at my own joke, but she doesn't laugh with me. "I'm going to find somewhere safe for you. I'm not going to hurt you," I offer.

"Why?"

"Because I'm not like Jerry. I don't believe in owning women, and you look like you could do with some help." Her expression had remained flat until my last comment, then her face flushed in anger.

"I can take care of myself. I don't need you," Sahara snapped. As quickly as it had appeared, her anger left her. "I'm sorry. That was rude of me."

I'm going to have to tread carefully here if I don't want to alienate her, so I just nod my head in agreement and carry on sipping my coffee. Her stomach rumbles loudly, echoing in the room. She quickly puts her hand over it, embarrassment apparent in the way she's holding herself.

"When did you last eat?" She doesn't look malnourished, but she doesn't look well fed either.

She pauses for a moment, looking to be deep in thought. "I, I can't remember," She admits. "What day is it?"

"It's the 12th." She looks at me blankly. "Sunday," I offer instead.

"It was a few days ago then."

I grind my teeth in anger. I wish Jerry was here now, so I could show him what I think of the way he treats his women.

"Do you think you could manage a bacon sandwich?" She doesn't answer straightaway and I inwardly curse myself for not asking her if she was a vegetarian.

"Go on then," she smiles in response. "I think I could give it a try."

I busy myself in the kitchen area, grateful for the excuse to escape the stilted conversation. It's only a temporary reprieve, but I need to get my head in order. There's something about Sahara that causes me to lose my rationality. If I want to keep her safe I can't afford to be this careless.

❦

For a slip of a girl she certainly enjoyed her food. I don't claim to be a great cook, but I guess when you haven't eaten in days anything tastes good.

"What happens now?" she asks, carefully wiping non-existent crumbs from her mouth. It's these small gestures that betray her refinement. She definitely isn't from Jerry's normal hunting ground.

"Now, we pack up and get back on the road. I need to find a safe phone to contact my friend Declan, I probably scared the hell out of him last night with that call as we escaped." I pause to run my hand through my hair. Declan would be halfway here already if he knew where here was. I need to let him know I'm okay. "I'll try and find some more suitable clothes for you and some toiletries and shit."

"Do we have to go on the bike?" There's a hint of fear in her voice.

"I'm sorry, it's the only option right now. Is that a problem?"

"No, no its fine." The tone of her response betrays her. It's anything but fine.

I glance at her feet, noticing for the first time that she's barefoot. What did she have on last night? She sees me looking and walks over to the bed where she bends down and retrieves a pair of heels. "These do?" she looks to me for approval.

"They're not perfect, but they'll do till we find you something more suitable." Her feet are far too small for any of my shoes. I've no idea where the hell I'm going to find a store that sells what she needs in this area. We're going to have to make do a little longer until I think of somewhere safe.

Packing up takes no time, a side effect of traveling light and living from a backpack for too many years. Guess it does have its benefits after all.

Having looked around the room one last time to make sure we've not left anything behind, we're on our way within minutes. The main road offers me two options, left or right. I feel like I should toss a coin, but then gambling is what got me into this situation in the first place. Shrugging my shoulders, I pick left.

I just hope I made the right decision.

3

Declan

"*D*eclan, I need you." Cam's voice sounds serious. I can hear shouting in the background and then the call ends, but not before I hear the sound of a gunshot.

"Cam!" I shout at the now dead phone. Holly moves towards me from the end of the bed where she's been sitting, but I push her away as I stand. I'm pacing the floor whilst redialing Cam's number. There's no response, just an annoying tone that's frustrating the hell out of me.

"Declan, what's wrong? You're scaring me." I'm frantic, trying to figure out what to do for my friend. I haven't got time to answer Holly, but I do.

"It's Cam, something's happened to him. He asked for my help and as the phone went dead I heard gun fire."

"Where is he? Do you need to go to him?" I love this girl;

she knows how much Cam means to me. He may not be my brother by birth, but he's as close as.

"I don't know where he is." Even as I'm talking to Holly I'm processing ideas. I can contact Chris; see if he can track the phone. I'm pretty sure he'll have some software he can use. Chris runs his own private security firm, I'm not sure where he gets his funding, all he'll say is it's not the bad guys, but he has access to some serious kit. He recently helped us out with a situation back in Severed. That guy has access to more advanced stuff than we were using over in Afghanistan. He's a walking military supermarket.

I pull Chris's speed dial up on my phone and tap my foot impatiently as the line rings.

"Declan?" Chris's sleepy voice answers. "Do you know what fekking time it is?" Actually, I've no idea, I'd kind of been distracted by Holly and her promise of hot sex. She's left the room, but reappears in the bathroom doorway, fastening a silk robe around her glorious nakedness. "I'm sorry," I whisper in her direction. She nods her acknowledgement of my apology, coming to stand close beside me. I draw her into me, finally replying to Chris.

"Sorry, Chris. Can't be helped. Cam's got involved in something that sounds serious, but his phone has died. Any chance you can track it for me and tell me where he is?" I'm hoping Chris can help.

"I'm sorry, Declan. I've got an app that tracks location for my guys, but it has to be installed on the phone first. What's he got, an iPhone?" I can hear the regret in Chris's voice.

"Yeah, an iPhone 8 I think."

"Can't be done mate. Even the FBI can't get Apple to release the code for that sort of search. That's why we use them ourselves."

"Is there no way of narrowing it down? Cam could be anywhere between here and Perth, that's over 3000 miles." Frustration is creeping into my voice, but fear is taking a grip on my heart. I can't lose Cam, not after everything we've been through. It's only Holly's grip tightening on my arm that stops me falling into the memory of that fateful mission in Afghanistan where our vehicle blew up and I ended up killing a teenage terrorist. I still have nightmares about it.

"I take it he was traveling home from Severed?" Chris asks.

"Yeah, he was on the bike, said he wanted to take his time going home and was going to stop off at a few different places on the way back." Cam had ridden with me across the coast from Perth to Severed just a few months ago. It was our way of trying to put the bad memories behind us after one of our team, Max, committed suicide. He'd lost his leg in the explosion that ended our tour of Afghanistan, and between that and the PTSD couldn't resist the lure of drugs. It had been a hard time for all of us after the accident, but we hadn't lost as much as Max. The poor sod couldn't see a way back from it all. I'd tried to lose myself in alcohol; it was Cam who'd suggested the road trip to help me regain control of my life. This is all my fault. I can't handle any more loss.

"Declan!" Chris has raised his voice; I must have missed whatever he was saying, lost in my thoughts.

"Sorry, Chris. Can you say that again?"

"Cam's solid. He's got a shit load of experience. He knows how to handle himself. Let's not worry till we know we have something to worry about. If his phone's dead he'll find another way of getting in touch with you."

Chris is right. Cam was my right-hand man over in Afghanistan, and he proved himself again when we had to tackle some drug dealing wannabes in Severed. I just feel so useless. I'm not even at home, I'd taken Holly away for a fucking romantic break to see if we could make it as a couple. I couldn't be any more ill prepared to help Cam right now.

"Yeah, you're right. Thanks, Chris. Sorry to have woken you up."

"Declan, you can lose that defeated tone right now," Chris admonishes. "Cam will get in touch and when he does I'm sure he'll be fine. That guy always comes up smelling of roses." I chuckle, he's right. Cam always has a way of coming out on top. "Let me know when you hear from him, and if you need anything, and I mean anything, you let me know." Chris feels he owes me after I rescued him from a mission that had gone tits up in Afghanistan. After all the help and equipment he gave us in Severed I'm pretty sure we're even, although I never thought there was a debt to be paid in the first place.

"Will do, and Chris, thanks for everything." I cut off the call and stare at my phone, willing it to ring. The blank screen taunts me.

"What do we do now?" Holly asks.

"We do nothing," I snap at her. "You're going home." As

soon as the words have left my mouth I regret them, not what I said, but the tone.

"Like hell I am, Declan," she huffs. "We're together now and you'd better get used to that. Wherever you go, I'm going." My girl's a hell cat, and most of the time that would turn me on, right now it scares the crap out of me. I can't see her get hurt. This is why I thought we shouldn't be together. Between my almost killing her during a nightmare, and this violent lifestyle I can't seem to escape, I worry that there's no future for us. Not that she sees it that way, she's fought me every step of the way, pushing her way into my life until I had to give in and accept it. Not now though, I can't let her be a part of whatever this is. The risk is too great.

Holly pulls us down to a sitting position on the edge of the bed, drawing me into a comforting embrace. "You need me, Declan. Let me be here for you," she pleads.

It's been over twelve hours since Cam called last night. I've watched every one of them tick by on the alarm clock at the side of the bed. My fully charged phone mocks me with its silence. Chris rang earlier; he's no closer to a solution than I am.

We've stayed in the cabin, as I've no idea which direction we'll need to head in when I hear from him. I'm reluctant to return to Severed, even though we're only a couple of hours away, in case it's the wrong direction.

Holly's tried to keep me from going insane bless her, but she can't ease away this nagging pain in my gut caused by the fear I'm going to lose Cam.

I almost drop my phone when it rings, an unknown number on the screen.

"Hello?" I answer hesitantly.

"Declan, thank fuck! It's taken me an hour to track your number down." He's alive. Relief floods my body; my knees go weak and I fall back into a seated position on the bed.

"Are you okay? You scared the shit out of me, Cam."

"It's a long story mate. I got myself into a bit of a mess last night. Any chance you can come give me a hand to sort it out?"

"Where are you? What do you need? What the fuck did you do?" I fire out the questions.

It takes Cam a good half hour to fill me in on the events of the previous night, and I'm not sure I fully understand what happened when he's finished relating it all. What I do know is he needs my help, and I'll move heaven and earth to get to him. Thankfully he's only a few hours away from here.

Once the call has ended I ring Chris and let him know where I'm heading and what I need for now. Holly's busy packing up our stuff in the background. I don't want to take her with me, but Cam asked for her. Turns out he's got some scared woman in tow and he thinks she may feel more comfortable and safer with Holly there.

I've no idea what shit Cam has got himself mixed up in, but I do know I'll do anything for him. We promised to always be there for each other and I'm going to uphold that promise.

4

Cam

*R*elief rushes through me as I hang up the call with Declan. He's only a couple of hours away and he's on his way.

The girl watches me when she thinks I can't see her. She's shown very little emotion, other than the hesitation when it came to getting on the bike, and I'm not sure that's healthy. That said, I'm pretty grateful she's not sniveling and bawling instead.

The roadside stop I've found to call Declan from has a basic shop attached. It's a tourist stop more than anything, but at least they had some decent walking shoes that fit her, as well as some jeans and a tacky souvenir hoodie that will keep her a little warmer and safer on the bike. I'm more comfortable about her safety now, although I'd have been happier if she'd been wearing leathers. The thought of her in black leather sends a twitch to my dick. I need to stop thinking of her in that way. It's not going to happen. She's nothing more than a job.

Declan's agreed to meet us a little closer to home, so it's going to be a few more hours on the road for us yet, and then a few more before he and Holly arrive. He was reluctant to bring Holly along, but as I explained, I don't speak 'woman', it might as well be a foreign language to me. Sure, I can charm a woman out of her pants and into my bed, but this girl needs more than that.

She's not showing it much, but I'm sure she's scared, and so she should be, not of me, but our situation. I'm not sure how much she knows about Jerry and what kind of man he is. He's a nobody in the grand scheme of things, but he's that dangerous kind of nobody who thinks he's somebody. His uncle on the other hand, that's a guy you don't mess with. His name is mentioned in awed whispers and with respect whereas Jerry is mentioned in ridicule. Jerry will use his uncle's reputation to get back what he's lost, and that means we need to watch our backs. His uncle's name carries a lot of weight and can unleash a mess of untold proportions. The challenge ahead of me makes Afghanistan look like a walk in the park.

I look around the quiet car park hoping that the next leg of the journey is quiet. Australia may be a vast country with a lot of unpopulated areas, but I don't want to stray too far off the main road back to Perth. I haven't got the right equipment, I think we're better off making good time and heading home where we can bunker up and defend ourselves against whatever Jerry throws our way.

I'm slightly surprised and very relieved that he hasn't found us yet. Whilst he's not the sharpest tool in the box, he does have his uncle's network to fall back on. I'm sure that at some point on our journey we'll show up on his radar.

He's a lazy fighter who doesn't like to get his own hands dirty, so I fully expect that he'll hire in some muscle to track us down.

The girl is walking back from the restroom, her long blonde hair tamed into a ponytail, the dark blue jeans tightly skimming her ass. It would look hot as hell if it weren't for the cartoon koala flashed across the front of her top. She looks like a dumb tourist, perfect.

When she gets to the bike she draws in a deep breath, looking at it with veiled fear. I need to get to the bottom of this, but right now's not the time. I help her onto the rear seat, passing her the leather jacket and waiting till she's fastened it securely before I get on in front of her. I'm glad now that I went for a touring bike, this would have been a hell of a painful journey on a sports bike with a rear passenger crushing my balls against the tank the whole way home.

I check the car park one last time before we set off, it doesn't look like anyone's even around, never mind watching us. I set off as steadily as I can so as not to alarm her. As I accelerate onto the main road I feel her grip tighten around my waist and I have to say it feels good.

The hotel that we're meeting at is understated but has a good diner attached. That's where we're sitting when Declan walks in. I stand to greet him, and he pulls me into a hug, I can see the relief on his face. Holly looks as gorgeous as ever; her shoulder length chocolate brown hair shines in the late afternoon sun streaming through the window. I can just see the odd hint of red, Declan's going to have to watch himself with her, I can just imagine how feisty she will be. My Mum's a red head and has given my Dad hell for as long as I can remember. I give her a hug and then make the awkward introductions, realizing that I can't recall the girls name again. Shit. I know it begins with S and is some fancy assed name. I pause as I introduce her and hope she'll fill in the gap. The silence becomes awkward before she realizes and answers for me.

"I'm Sahara," she introduces herself.

"What an unusual name, it's very pretty," Holly offers.

"I used to be Sarah, but Jerry didn't think it was exotic enough to raise a good price, so he changed it." She says it with no emotion; did we just hear her right?

"Did you just say you were going to be sold?" I ask, my voice betraying my anger. Declan looks like he's about to blow and Holly's just sitting there with shock on her face. "Who was he selling you to? I thought you were with him?" I almost stutter over the last two questions.

"The highest bidder of course." Her voice is so unemotional; you'd think we were discussing something from TV, not the trafficking of people. I don't even want to think of the kind of person Jerry would have sold her to. "Jerry wanted to sample the goods before he sold me, so I was his till he grew tired of me."

"How long...?" I can't finish the question.

"Last night would have been my first night with him."

For the first time I can hear something in her voice, her words were said through quivering lips. A lone tear makes its way down her cheek, almost breaking me. Holly moves in closer to her and pulls her into a hug.

"Wouldn't you rather we call you Sarah?" Holly offers.

"No, Sarah belongs to another life, a life I'll never get back." The flat, matter of fact way she says it causes Holly's eyes to become teary as well. There's a story here, and I'm determined to get to the bottom of it.

"You're going to be okay now, Sahara," Holly promises. "My wounded heroes will protect you."

Declan and I look at her, jaws dropping. "What the fuck did you just call us?" Declan splutters.

"You're my wounded heroes." She smiles. "You came back from Afghanistan broken, but you're my heroes for saving my family back in Severed, so I call you my wounded heroes."

I almost want to laugh at the silly nickname she's given us, but I don't. We may not be heroes, but she's right. We all came back from that place wounded in one way or another. We just don't all have the physical scars to show from it.

Sahara wipes away the tear, a small smile appearing on her face at Holly's explanation. "That would be nice, no one's ever protected me before." Holly tightens her hug.

"Well, girl, that's all about to change," she promises. Holly eyes Sahara up and down. "Now, first, we need to get some food into you, you don't look like you've had a decent meal in forever, and then... then we need to do something about that god-awful hoody you're wearing."

Like I said, Holly is going to be a force to be reckoned with.

5

Cam

*D*uring the course of the meal Sahara has said very little. Holly tried to pump her for information, whilst Declan and I listened. She didn't say much more than what we already know. Jerry had pursued her for a while, she'd rejected his offers for as long as she could until he pulled some strings and made her both homeless and jobless. Sahara said this was the point where she had nothing left and nowhere to go, and with no other options available, she ended up with Jerry.

Sahara told us that he'd kept her in some kind of secure safe house with a bunch of other girls, who gradually disappeared one by one, although new girls were arriving all the time. From what she'd been able to pick up on the grapevine, the girls were being sold to order, and to some not very nice people. She'd overheard that not all the girls survived their new owners.

"Fuck," Holly whispers. "This sounds like the bloody plot of a Lily White book." We all look at her, no idea what's she's talking about. "She's an author I read who writes some really dark shit. It sounds like human trafficking to me. I didn't think that kind of stuff happened here." Her voice betrays the horror she is feeling.

"Sadly, it happens everywhere." Declan tells her. "It's a huge billion-dollar industry. You hear about tourists being kidnapped to order whilst they're on holiday, or girls being snatched from their college dorm because they fit the profile of a particular buyer." A shudder runs through Holly.

Holly's about to ask more questions when Sahara stops her. "Please? I really don't want to talk about it anymore right now." The poor girl has hardly touched her food. She's been doing that thing that kids do, moving food around on the plate to make it look like she's eating, when in reality hardly anything has passed her lips.

"It's okay, Sahara," I reassure her. "We'll give it a rest, but we do need to talk about this more at some point. We need to know exactly what we're up against so that we can protect you."

"Why?" She sounds surprised. "Why do you want to protect me?"

"Because that's what we do," I simply reply.

Holly and Sahara are in the adjoining room, drinking hot chocolate and having 'girl time' as Holly calls it. She's promised Sahara she won't hit her with questions all night. In reality she's just trying to fill her up with popcorn and marshmallows, hoping to get her to eat something. She's looking like she's in need of a good meal as well as being exhausted at the moment.

Declan is in my room and we're trying to work out what we're up against. I'm still struggling to work out how I got myself into this bloody mess. I only wanted a game of poker for God's sake.

"So, you reckon this Jerry guy won't let this drop?"

"Not a chance in hell, Declan." I explain a little about Jerry's background. "Jerry is the local enforcer, working on behalf of his family, although I'm pretty sure his Uncle doesn't know half the shit he pulls. You know his Uncle, its Jack's Dad."

Declan's so shocked he repeats my words, "His uncle's Jack Snr?" he groans.

"One and the same," I offer. Jack Snr isn't a stranger to us. His son served with us out in Afghanistan but didn't make it. He'd died in my arms and had given me a last message to pass on to his father. Walking into that room after the funeral and passing that message on was one of the hardest things I've ever had to do. I'd rather walk into a room full of armed insurgents than do that again.

"Would he back Jerry against you, everything considered?" Declan questions.

"I honestly don't know. Jerry is part of his family after all. Family means everything to those guys. Let's put it this way, it's not a gamble I'd want to take."

"You need to go see him if we can't sort this out ourselves." Declan suggests. "He might not know about it, he may not even condone it. Blood is one thing, but a lot of these families have principles as well."

I really don't know which way Jack Snr would go. For all I know he's involved, although it doesn't match with the guy I think I know. I've been invited back to social gatherings when I've not been on tour, so I know there's some connection there, but I seriously doubt it's strong enough to beat that of a blood relation.

"He's not the bloody mafia, Declan." I laugh.

"No, but he's related to them." He's right, and that sobers me up a little. With Jerry's family connections I think I may well have bitten off more than I can handle this time.

"Do we need to call the guys in?" Declan offers. The rest of our 'wounded heroes' all went back to their day jobs after the incident in Severed, but they promised to be there again if we needed them.

"Not yet, I don't want to drag them into this if I don't have to."

"I've spoken to Chris and he's sending us some gear." Declan grins like a kid anticipating Father Christmas arriving. Chris is a veritable one-man military supermarket, and he only has the best. I dread to think what Declan means by 'gear'. "It'll be here in the morning." Chris had kitted us out for our last adventure back in Severed, I remember the way Declan spoke in awe of the warehouse he'd visited. He'd looked like a kid who'd been let loose in a sweet shop as he described the high-tech kit we'd never had available to us in Afghanistan. Seems like private venture is definitely the way to go, Chris has a flourishing business although he still won't tell us who his clients are.

"You decent in there?" Holly's voice rings out, accompanied by a tuneful rapping on the connecting door. When Declan opens it, the girls are just on the other side. "Sahara's exhausted, she needs her bed," Holly grins at Declan as she continues, "and I need my man."

Declan gives me a shit eating grin and a wave as he heads back into the other room. I point Sahara in the direction of her twin bed and offer her the use of the bathroom first; I'm a gentleman after all. She gives me a tired smile, gathers up the toiletry bag that Holly made up for her and heads off to freshen up. Her vulnerability is eating at me. She's had a shitty time with Jerry, and right now we don't know if it's about to get better or worse.

Whilst she's in the shower I sit on my own twin and try second guessing Jack Snr. Declan's right, I may need to go talk to him, but I want to avoid it as long as possible. I know it's only the second day, but we've not seen any of Jerry's goons yet. I know we were followed, I could hear the screech of tires in pursuit. I can't see Jerry giving up a prize like Sahara, especially if he had a buyer lined up for when he'd finished with her. I bristle with rage at the thought of Sahara being manhandled by Jerry, and probably someone much worse. I can't get my head around her ending up in a situation like this, she seems such a normal girl. Then again, that probably makes her more valuable an asset for Jerry. Maybe I'm overthinking the whole thing. Maybe Jerry won't be out to exact revenge.

Maybe pigs really do fly. On that thought my head hits the pillow and I'm out for the count.

6

Cam

The sun is streaming through the gap in the curtains when I wake up. I'm a little disorientated at first, then when I see the empty bed at the side of me I shoot up, panic rushing through me. Relief filters slowly in as I hear the sound of women's laughter through the open door connecting us to Declan's room.

"Look what the cat dragged in." Declan laughs as I enter, barefoot and wearing just my jeans. I scrub a hand through my hair and realize it's sticking out all over the place.

"Yeah, whatever," I ignore him as I head for the pot of coffee I can smell, seeking it out and pouring a large mug for myself. I almost inhale the first cup before coming up for air and seeing three pairs of inquisitive eyes watching me. "Sorry, guys. I needed that." I laugh.

"We could tell." Holly giggles. Sahara is sat cross-legged on the sofa next to her, wearing the oversized koala hoodie I bought her and not a lot else from what I can see. She's watching what's going on, but she's still not joining in the conversation.

"What time is it?" I question, looking at my empty wrist; my watch must be on the bedside table.

"10am," Declan informs me. "You were out for the count, so we let you sleep."

I guess I needed it after the last couple of days. It must have been adrenalin that had kept me going for a while there.

"Chris's guys should be here any time," Declan continues. "They're dropping off a vehicle for us with some supplies and they're sending a truck to collect the bikes."

Sahara's face shows relief at the promise of a change in transport. I make a mental note to find out why she's so scared of my bike. It seems to be much more than first time nerves, and the way she held herself on the back of the bike tells me she's been a passenger on one before.

I've not finished my second coffee before we hear a vehicle pull up outside, closely followed by a knock at the door. Declan looks through the peephole, his gun ready at his side. Grinning widely, he opens the door and beckons me over. "Santa's arrived."

Chris has sent us a huge four by four and the boot is laden with weapons, handguns, sniper rifles, army knives, even a few smoke bombs and grenades. I love that guy. Declan also sorted out some cash for us, so we don't have to use our credit cards or bank accounts and can stay off the radar.

From the look of the bundle he's thumbing through he managed to arrange for a lot of cash.

Once we've checked everything and repacked it we say goodbye to the courier. He informs us the truck will be by in an hour to pick up the bikes, so I grab a shower and shave before we quickly pack the rest of our stuff then head over to the diner for a late breakfast. I don't know about anyone else but I'm starving.

I almost groan in pleasure as I place a forkful of bacon in my mouth from my overflowing extra large breakfast platter. Declan has the same as me, but the girls have both gone for melon, cereal and juice. I haven't had my full fix of coffee yet, so managed to persuade the young waitress to leave me the pot.

Sahara eats a little more this morning, and I think she seems a touch less wary of us. She's still not at ease though. She's constantly watching what's going on around her. I thought at first, she was just a people watcher like me, but its more than that. She looks ready to run at any moment, flinching every time the door opens to let in a new customer. I thought Declan and I were alert, but she's hyper vigilant.

I've got a mouth full of bacon and egg when she lets out a gasp and goes white. She's looking out of the window, so I turn to see what she's spotted. All I see are a couple of guys getting out of a beat-up old Ford truck, nothing unusual about that. When I look more closely I recognize one of the men, it's one of Jerry's guys. Shit. I thought we had more of a head start.

He's pointing excitedly at my bike as I hurriedly rise from the table, my cutlery falling to the floor with a clash and earning looks of distrust from the few other diners that are in here. Declan catches my eye and quickly follows. I'm watching the two jerks all the time as I rush from the diner, not fast enough to stop them as they start firing at my bike. It all feels like it's happening in slow motion. Before I can reach them, a bullet has caught the petrol tank and my bike goes up with a huge explosion. Fuck! The bikes are too close together and Declan's bike goes up next. Black smoke rising above the flames as the fuel burns fiercely.

Gun in hand, I raise my arm and fire off shot after shot. Out of the corner of my eye I can see Declan has his gun raised and is firing as well. I can't stop the vehicle from peeling out of the car park, but I do get a small amount of satisfaction when I see the rear windscreen shatter and blood cover the passenger window when my next bullet finds its target. The Ford pulls away from us, even though we're fit, our running speed is no match for the old truck.

"Fuck, fuck, fuck!" I curse. I can't get near the bikes for the flames. I feel a small hand in mine. It's Sahara. Again, a lone tear rolls down her cheek as she turns to me.

"I'm sorry," she whispers. "I'm so sorry." What the fuck is she apologizing for? I quickly pull her into my side and start moving us toward the truck.

There's chaos behind us as several staff and patrons are passing water in bowls and cups between them, trying to extinguish the flames. Hopefully the bikes were parked far enough away from the building that the diner won't catch fire. We should stay and help, but right now our priority is Sahara and getting her out of here. I don't think the local police would take too kindly to the arsenal we're transporting right now.

Declan has our truck running and the passenger doors open. Holly is already strapped into the back seat and he shouts for us to hurry up and join them. I'm so glad we packed everything up before we went to the diner. Thankfully the two goons hadn't realized that the truck was ours, or that Declan was with me. They'll think that they've destroyed my bike and I'm stuck here now. Watching my bike burn I'm not so sure that luck is on my side.

I hustle Sahara into the back seat, next to Holly, and yell at her to fasten her seatbelt. As soon as I jump into the passenger seat, before I can even pull the door shut and block out the screams and shouts from the customers in the diner, Declan has the four by four burning rubber and heading in the opposite direction down the highway.

It looks like Jerry does want revenge after all.

7

Cam

"What the hell...?" I'm lost for words as the truck rushes down the highway, Declan at the wheel.

"I didn't think Jerry would have caught up with you so quickly," Declan replies. "What do you want to do now?"

If it was just Declan and me I wouldn't need to think about it, I'd have been hot on the trail of the arsehole that just shot up my bike, then going in search of Jerry. But it's not just us. We've got the girls to think about now. I turn to check on them in the back seat. Holly doesn't look too phased by what's just happened; I guess that comes from having a brother in an MC. Had a brother in an MC, I remind myself. Sahara on the other hand looks white and shaken, although Holly is doing her best to comfort her.

"I say we find this Jerry guy and beat the crap out of him,"

Holly offers. She says it as though she were discussing a day out, not a potential bloody war zone.

"That's my girl!" Declan laughs. "But seriously, what do you want to do?"

My gut instinct tells me I need to go talk to Jack Snr, now before it's too late. I tend to trust my instincts, as they've saved my life on more than one occasion. Whatever he decides at least I'll know where I stand.

"Let's get the girls somewhere safe, then I'll go see Jack."

"You sure?" Declan looks at me.

"Yeah, you never know he might surprise us." Jack's an honorable guy, but Jerry's family. This one's too close to call.

"You want me to come with you?"

"Best not, just in case," I tell him. "Drop me off nearby, if anything goes wrong at least you can take care of the girls."

Declan nods in agreement. We spend the next hour working out the best route to Jerry, and the safest point in between for the girls. Holly, typical woman, reminds us that there's a huge shopping mall midway and that she and Sahara can get lost in it quite easily for a couple of hours. Declan groans when Holly suggests using some of the money Chris left us to get the girls some new clothes. I just laugh. Holly has him by the balls already, even if he doesn't realize it.

The shopping mall is huge, Holly's right; it's a good place for the girls to get lost in for a few hours while we're gone. Declan and I have been on alert the whole way here looking for any sign we're being followed and there was nothing. We also headed in the opposite direction to the one we think Jerry's guys went when they took off.

We park in a quiet corner of the car park, we don't need anyone seeing our cargo of weapons, or the stash of money that Chris supplied us with. As discreetly as he can Declan grabs a couple of bundles of twenties and passes them to Holly. Her handbag is so large she has more than enough room for them to disappear, as well as the pistol Declan insists on giving her. He hands her one of the burner mobiles once he's made a note of the number. We'd destroyed our own sim cards before breakfast, one less thing to be able to track us with. I can't help wondering if our delay in doing that could have led Jerry to us, but then again, I'm not sure he's intelligent enough to have thought of that.

Holly's face lights up as she approaches the front door of the mall, Sahara looks a lot less enthusiastic.

When she sees me watching her she shrugs her shoulders, "Guess I'm just not used to being around a lot of people anymore." She tries to smile and look more confident for me, but I can see past it. She's far too young to be carrying such troubles. I need to get to the bottom of what she's been through, so I can help her heal.

We're barely through the door before Holly lets out a high-pitched squeal and drags Sahara along by the hand to a shop window. Looking closer it's a shoe shop. She's spotted something.

Holly is gushing over a pair of obscenely high heels, they must be at least five-inch heels. How the hell do women walk in those things? With their pointed toes they look like torture devices, not a fashion accessory.

Before I've had chance to open my mouth and protest we're in the store and Holly has a young male sales assistant fawning over her. His eyes light up when she mentions the shoes from the window. I look at Declan and he shakes his head, he has no idea what's going on either. We just let her get on with it.

The young guy comes back with a shoebox, carrying it as though it's a precious cargo or an unexploded bomb. Holly fawns over the shoes inside. Really? They're just a pair of shoes. As she's trying on the shoes I pick up the empty box, holy shit, is that price for real? She can't be serious. I've spent less on a leather jacket than she's proposing to spend on the most impractical shoes I've ever seen. At least they're leather I grumble to myself as I put the offending shoebox down.

Holly's showing off the shoes to Sahara who looks almost as lost as me over the attraction. Sahara heads over to a sale display rack and picks up the ugliest pair of sensible shoes I've ever seen. "Seriously?" I ask her, looking at them in disgust.

"But they're only $10," she replies. She's been used to spending money thriftily I suspect, rather than on a whim.

Having noted the size of the shoe in her hand I suggest a more attractive, yet still sensible pair from a different display. She can run in these if she needs to, but they don't look like something your Great Aunt Agatha would wear! She goes even whiter when she sees the price, but the $100 ticket is a fraction of what Holly's looking to spend.

"Just try them on." I pass her the shoes.

They fit perfectly, and despite their practicality, they look great on the end of her long jean clad legs. I take them back from her and head to the till to pay for them. Holly however has no intention of buying just the one pair of shoes, much to Declan's chagrin, and he has to almost frog march her to the till. I let out a too loud laugh that earns me a glare from Holly.

Apparently, Declan has appeased her by reminding her she has several hours to kill and a whole shopping mall to explore.

A few stores further in there's a coffee shop and we head there. Over coffee and cheesecake, we explain to the girl's where we're going, what time we're hoping to be back to pick them up, and more importantly, how to contact Chris if anything happens to us.

"Is it really that dangerous going to see Jack Snr?" Sahara looks frightened.

"My gut says not, but better to be safe than sorry," I reply.

"I'm sorry that I got you into my mess." Sahara looks crestfallen.

"Don't apologize. I'm always happy to help a gorgeous damsel in distress," I smile at her.

The poor girl blushes and tries to hide her face from me.

When was the last time someone paid her a compliment? I'm not sure where this is going to go once we've sorted out the problem with Jerry, but I do hope she'll give me a chance to show her that the world isn't full of arseholes.

⚜

Too soon the coffee stop has ended and we're saying goodbye to the girls. It's time to head and see Jack Snr.

The next few hours could go either way. I'd like to think that I'll come through this, and that I'm a good enough judge of character, but Afghanistan left me so full of doubt. I haven't told Declan, but I still have nightmares about that last day. I put on a good act, but there's a constant cloud of dread hanging over me. Something bad is going to happen, I just don't know what, or when.

8

Cam

Pulling up outside the house I realize what a risk I'm taking by coming here, but I can't see any other option right now. I need this guy onside. The house exudes money, in a tasteful way. The neatly lawned garden, crystal clear water in the stone fountain, and the perfectly trimmed olive trees either side of the door all testament to a property that's been well maintained.

The heavy that opens the front door doesn't look like a butler, although I wouldn't have been surprised to see one in a property of this size. His large neck almost doesn't fit in the collar of his crisp white shirt. He's not fat though, he's solidly built. I wouldn't want to come across him on a dark night that's for sure. I may have the element of speed due to my lighter weight, but one punch from him and it wouldn't matter how fast I can run.

"Cam," he greets me, his deep voice showing no emotion. I

can't even get a clue from his tone how this meeting's going to go down. Today is either going to turn out to be a good decision or a very bad one. I'm hoping for the former. I can't remember the guy's name, so I just nod my greeting and follow him when he indicates.

For all Jack's wealth this place still has a homely feel about it, which I'm guessing is down to his wife Natasha's influence. There's none of the gaudy gold-plated plaster and alabaster you get in some of these grand houses, instead the walls are a cream color that captures and reflects the light, making it bright and welcoming. The walls of the hallway are lined with family images. I stop in front of one showing a young guy in military uniform. Jack Jnr. The reason I'm hopeful of walking out of here alive.

The heavy opens a door up ahead on the left and ushers me in. Jack Snr is seated behind a large walnut desk, like the rest of the house the furniture is functional and comfortable rather than ostentatious. He rises and comes around the desk to meet me.

"Good to see you again, Cam." He greets me warmly, his handshake firm but friendly. That's a good sign. Once we've exchanged token pleasantries about the weather he shows me to a seating area in front of the fireplace, offering me a drink. I decline; I need to keep my wits about me for this conversation.

"I hear you've got yourself into a bit of a mess, Cam. Care to explain?" That one sentence tells me all I need to know. He knows why I'm here, what I've done, and who I've upset. I still can't gauge how he's feeling about the situation.

"I had a bit of a run in with Jerry, your nephew, Sir." Whilst he's told me to call him Jack since our first meeting, I think this situation calls for a show of respect. He takes a sip of his expensive whisky, taking a moment to savor the taste before swallowing. He says nothing, just looks at me, so I continue.

"I'm not sure if you know all of the activities he's got himself involved in," I start, hoping to let him know I don't think he's involved, "but his latest venture seems to have caused some friction between us." I pause. How do you tell someone that you suspect their nephew is involved in human trafficking, especially when you haven't got the evidence to back it up yet? "It came to light after we had a game of poker and I won. Jerry bet something he didn't want to lose and now he wants it back." I pause again. I'm nervous. Put me in a battlefield and I'm fine. Put me in front of this guy, and I'm hesitant. Part of it comes from the respect I have for him, both as a father and a businessman. It's the businessman I need to be wary of; one word from him can see me destroyed.

"You don't want to give it back?" Jack asks. "I guess if you won it fair and square then no one should expect you to." His voice is calm, reasoned. I still can't read how this is going to go.

"It's not the winning that bothers me. It's what will happen to it if I give it back that's stopping me," I reply carefully. We're dancing around the subject and I need to be blunter or we'll be here all afternoon.

"Jerry bet a girl." I wait a moment to let this sink in. "If he gets her back I'm afraid between him and his 'buyers' she'll be destroyed, I don't think she'll endure what they have planned for her." It sounds so melodramatic, but it's the truth. If Jerry gets his hands on Sahara she's not strong enough to survive the ordeal he'll put her through.

"What do you mean 'buyers'?" Jack asks.

"I've done a bit of digging and it turns out that Jerry set himself up as a pimp, but he's taken it further. He's stealing girls to order now. His clients aren't fussy about where the girls come from, and several of the girls he's sold have been found dead. "

Jack looks at me. His face is still unreadable, but I'm almost sure there was a twitch of his lips when I mentioned girls dying. "Go on."

"From what I can tell, and its still very early intel, Jerry has some buyers with some pretty hardcore tastes. They pay big money for him to supply girls and ask no questions. It's more than just pimping, it's trafficking I believe."

Jack slams his fist down on to the small walnut side table, which shakes under the force. "Greg!" He shouts, summoning the guy who answered the door to me.

"Yes, Boss?" Greg stands to attention in front of us.

"You heard any rumors about Jerry and some girls?" Jack questions.

Greg shifts uncomfortably. "Nothing I've been able to prove, Boss."

Jack looks between us. "How come this is the first I'm hearing of it?" His voice doesn't hold anger, but it's not far off it.

"Probably for the same reason I hesitated to come here and

talk to you, lack of evidence," I offer. "So far everything I've heard is hearsay." Greg nods in agreement.

"So why have you come to me?" Jack asks.

"Because I respect you, Sir," I hesitate, "and because if Jerry doesn't stop trying to get her back I'm pretty sure one of us will end up dead." As far as I'm concerned, it's going to be Jerry, but even I'm not foolish enough to be that blunt in front of his uncle.

"And?" Jack asks. "There's more to it than that I'm sure."

"Because, Sir, if I'm the one that comes out of this alive, I'd very much like for you not to kill me in retaliation."

Jack chuckles at my bold statement. Greg says nothing, but I can see from the sparkle in his eye that he finds my comment amusing as well.

"Cam, you know I would do anything for you, you were there with my son when he died in that god-awful place, you came and shared his last moments with my wife and I after you tried to save his life. But Jerry's my flesh and blood," he sounds so disappointed, "unfortunately."

Jerry and his uncle are chalk and cheese. Where one holds ultimate power and respect, the other is ridiculed. Jerry plays on his uncle's name and connections to get by in life. I'm relying on that to get me through this.

"Boss," Greg starts, "what happens if we stay out of it, let these two sort it out themselves? Everyone knows you won't have any part in trafficking." Greg has voiced my own thoughts.

"I won't. It's abhorrent." Jack answers. "Jerry grew up in my home, I raised him alongside Jack Jnr like a son. My wife would never forgive me if I condoned anything." Disappointment laces his voice.

"Don't be so sure of that." A soft-spoken voice breaks the silence. All our heads turn to the office door as it pushes open. "You should be more careful to keep your door shut, darling." A beautiful brunette walks in, the embodiment of style and grace.

"Cam, lovely to see you again." She greets me with a kiss on each cheek before turning to her husband.

"If Jerry's dealing in trafficking then he deserves everything he gets," Natasha declares to her husband. "I'll cry no tears over that boy. You gave him every chance, every opportunity. As you say, you raised those boys as if they were both your sons. One lies dead thanks to some foreign battlefield, and the other has disrespected your name and our family with his actions. As far as I'm concerned the wrong son died that day."

Natasha walks over to sit on the arm of her husband's chair, her hand patting his as she talks. "There's no honor in selling women. If that boy is involved then show me the evidence and I'll give you my blessing, Cam." She surprises us all with her statement. Even Jack looks taken aback.

"I've always left you to head the family business," she kisses her husband on the cheek before rising from the arm of the chair, "but this is a family decision before a business one. Don't let a misplaced sense of loyalty stop you from doing what's right." She nods a polite goodbye to Greg and me as she leaves the room.

I'm kind of shocked. Jack Snr runs a formidable enterprise,

most of it legitimate, but not all of it. If this was Italy he'd be a mafia don, his family tree links him back to some formidable Italian families. Jack's always been careful about what business he was involved in, a bit of drug dealing, gun running and protection, but he's always stayed away from vice. I never thought of him as a man who'd take advice from his wife though.

Looking at Jack I realize he's not the man I first met, although that was only a few years ago, he's aged considerably. It doesn't show until you look closely, fine lines at the side of his eyes, which appear duller than they used to be unless his wife walks in the room, and then they light up. The loss of his son has obviously hit him hard.

Jack finishes the whisky in his glass in one go. Standing he moves towards me, offering his hand.

"Do what you need to do, Cam," he offers, sadness in his voice. "Just make sure you're 100% sure first, and I don't want him found, ever!" With that Jack turns and exits the room, leaving just Greg and me.

"You heard the Boss," Greg says. "Let's go have a chat and see if I know anything you don't." Greg leads me down to the basement kitchen where he pours me a glass of bourbon.

I call Declan to come and join us, and between the three of us we spend the rest of the afternoon discussing what we think we know, trying to work out how to prove it and the best way to act on it.

9

Declan

It felt like I'd waited forever for the call from Cam to let me know it had gone okay. Greg seems like a pretty switched on guy, I guess he's one of those who is always in the background and you forget he's there. All the time he's watching and listening. He knows far more than his boss realizes. He'd be a good guy to have watching your back. It's also obvious pretty soon into the conversation that Greg has no love for Jerry.

"He's a spineless, lazy bastard," Greg curses. "He'll hang on his uncle's coattails as long as he can." He pauses to take a sip of his bourbon. "Jack Jnr was twice the man he is, and then some."

We clink our glasses together in a toast to Jack Jnr.

Greg used to be in the military, so we share a few stories with each other from our time in Afghanistan. Even Greg gets a haunted look in his eyes when he recalls some of the less savory memories. I don't think anyone ever comes back from there the same person they were when they went.

The afternoon has flown past, I hadn't realized how late it had got until my phone rang and I saw the time. It's Gran's number. I haven't spoken to her in a few days, but right now it's not a good time so I hit the decline button. Seconds later the phone rings again, it's the same number so I hit decline. The third time it rings I answer it, wondering what can be so important she has to speak to me.

"Hi, Gran. What's up?" I smile into the phone, forgetting she can't see me. "Declan, its Fred from the farm. I'm sorry to have to ring you but you need to come home, your Gran's had a stroke and they're taking her to the hospital."

Something must show on my face as immediately both Greg and Cam look at me with concern. "What? When? How?" I stutter into the phone.

I listen carefully as Fred tries to explain. He'd come in from working with the horses to find Gran slumped in her chair, her china teacup shattered on the floor. She was conscious but couldn't talk and had left side weakness. The medivac helicopter had responded quickly, and although they weren't sure how long it had been since the stroke, they were fairly hopeful they'd got to her in time. The tea in the shards of the cup had still been warm.

She's being airlifted to the Royal Perth Hospital, which has a specialist stroke unit. Fred explains that they won't be able to tell us anymore until she's arrived and been assessed, but she'd lost consciousness by the time the helicopter took off. The helicopter has only just taken off and he and his wife are heading to the hospital to be with her, there wasn't room for them on the medivac.

I silently curse myself for not ringing her over the past few days. She's 90 years old and practically raised me, I should have taken better care of her, but she's a stubborn old woman at times and had insisted that I take on the challenge of running the pub in Severed. She has a good team working for her on the farm and was adamant that she'd be fine. Guilt is flowing through me. I assure Fred I'll be there as soon as I can. When I hang up I quickly explain what's happened to Greg and Cam. Greg surprises me by immediately offering me the use of Jack's private jet. I'm about to refuse when Cam reminds me that it's the quickest way to get to her.

"Thanks Greg, that's very kind of you." My hand as I go to shake his is trembling. I've survived being blown up in battle, and yet it only takes one phone call to reduce me to this shaking wreck. I can't imagine a world without Gran in it; she's always been there.

I've obviously drifted off in my thoughts as Cam touching my arm startles me. "We need to go get the girls, Declan," he reminds me.

"I need to get to Gran," I respond, my voice quiet and shaken.

"I know mate, but we're coming with you. You're not going through this on your own," he says, his voice taking on a comforting tone. "She's my family too." Cam adores Gran, there's a special bond between them, the pair of them often ganging up together against me.

"By the time you get to the landing strip the jet will be

ready for you," Greg advises. "Besides, Harvey is far enough away that hopefully Jerry won't be able to find you," he finishes. He has a point. Harvey will be a good place to hide away until we know what's happening, but right now I can't think about Jerry, I need to get to my Gran.

Cam is already on the phone with Holly when we reach the car. He declines my offer to drive, it's probably for the best, and I'm really not with it right now.

As we drive back to the shopping mall my mind replays memories, it's like watching one of those time reel videos on Facebook. Gran picking me up when I fell off my bike when I was learning to ride, gently cleaning the gravel rash from my knees. Gran standing stoically beside me at Granddad's funeral, a single tear tracking down her face. Gran's frail frame wrapping me in a tight hug I thought was going to suffocate me when I came home after the explosion in Afghanistan, and finally Gran threatening me when I was in my whisky induced seclusion, giving me the strength to get back up on my feet. She's always been there for me, and I realize that in the majority of memories that's how it was, she was there for me, and far too infrequently was I there for her. I need to get to her and put that right. This woman is my life.

The girls are ready and waiting for us outside the shopping mall, their faces somber, and offering words that are full of condolences.

"She's not dead yet!" I snap at them, then swiftly apologize. "I'm sorry, I shouldn't take it out on you. I know you're just concerned for her, but I can't stand being this far away."

Holly pats my arm reassuringly, "It's okay, babe. We understand. We'll be there soon."

Cam is driving fast, and in no time we're at the landing strip. As promised the jet is fueled and ready for us. Greg's there to greet us and introduce us to the crew.

"They'll get you there as soon as they can," he reassures me, "in the meantime, don't even think about Jerry, leave that with me. You've got more important things to worry about." Greg's taken care of putting our few belongings on the plane, although we're going to have to leave the weapons behind.

"Thanks for everything, Greg," Cam answers for us all. I'm still numb as we taxi down the runway, unaware of the opulent luxury of the plane we have found ourselves in, although the girls seem to be relishing it from the constant excited chatter.

The expected flight time is two hours, and I sit back in the seat knowing that this is going to be the longest two hours of my life.

10

Cam

*D*eclan is a nervous wreck the whole of the short flight. His knees are shaking with nervous energy. I know how close he is to his Gran, and hope to God that she's going to be okay. I can't bear to think what losing her would do to him, he's still hurting from what happened in Afghanistan and losing Max.

Holly and Sahara are sitting a few rows back, chatting quietly from the look of it. They're looking at the purchases they made at the mall, although the pile of bags next to Holly looks suspiciously larger than the couple of bags next to Sahara.

Fred's going to meet us at the airport and take Declan straight to the hospital, and I'm renting a pick up and taking Sahara back to the farm. The fewer people who see us together the better. I don't know who's in Jerry's pocket after all.

Sahara appears to be a little more relaxed since Holly joined us, although I can see the strain on her face still. I wonder what her story is? What's obvious is she's had a tough time, but my gut instinct tells me I should help her, that deep down she's good people. It looks like life has dealt her a pretty lousy hand.

Declan stays silent for the whole of the flight, his knee continuing to shake, although his foot never leaves the floor. His hands fidget in his lap. He's lost deep in thought, so I decide to leave him be, hoping he's not lost in memories of Afghanistan.

He's struggled more than the rest of us, blaming himself for what happened out there. He's not to blame. He wasn't the one who placed the IUD. I was the idiot who drove over it. His guilt over shooting the child eats at him, but he's got to get the idea out of his head that he was an innocent. As young as he was, he was a cold-hearted terrorist who was prepared to kill us all. Declan didn't take a life that day, he saved several.

Max's suicide hit everyone hard. To an extent we all failed him, although I'm not sure what we could have done to prevent it. We couldn't restore his leg, amputated after the explosion. We couldn't give him back the military career that was his life, he was the only one of us who had been going to re-enlist after that tour. We could perhaps have visited him in the hospital and at home more frequently, been aware of the drug addiction that was developing. We should have seen the signs. We were as close to him as anyone, but we let him push us away. I'm not going to let Declan push me away anymore, I'm not prepared to lose another friend to suicide.

I haven't told Declan, but I've had a few counseling sessions myself. I found them helpful. I really should tell him, it's not like it's a secret. I just don't want to give him any more ammunition in his journey of self-destruction. He feels enough of a failure. His counseling sessions haven't helped him, yet. I'm hopeful that he will find peace through them, and I know he wants to try so he can have a future with Holly. She's been good for him. She's also a strong enough character to stand up to him when needed. I'm sure between us we can help him, at least I hope we can.

I'm worried about the effect his Gran's stroke will have on his already fragile mental health. I pray she pulls through, she's an amazing old lady and one of the strongest people I know. I also know first-hand how destructive strokes can be. I lost my own gran to one. Declan's Gran is special to me, she took me under her wing and made me feel like one of her own. I don't think I can go through that loss again.

The seatbelt sign comes on as we prepare to land. Let's hope we're landing to good news.

※

D eclan and Holly head for the hospital with Fred as soon as the plane lands. Fred's given me a key to the farmhouse and told Sahara and I to make ourselves at home. He and his wife live in a cottage on the farm and the rest of the farmhands come in daily or stay in a bunkhouse, so it will just be the two of us.

Other than a brief conversation where we both hope Declan will receive good news when he gets to the hospital, most of the journey to the farm passes in silence. We're both lost in our own thoughts.

It's only when we reach the farm we realize how little shopping Sahara managed. It seems that Holly kept dragging her into expensive shops she just didn't feel comfortable in. She hasn't got any nightwear yet. Lending her one of my shirts I promise her we'll go get her the rest of the things she needs in the morning. The look of horror on her face has me swiftly offering Holly's services instead. Holly's more than happy to assist when I text her.

There's no news yet regarding Gran, she's still unconscious and it's too early to have a prognosis. Declan's staying at the hospital with her and Holly has booked them into a hotel over the road, so he has a room close by when he needs it.

Sahara makes us a simple meal, neither of us is particularly hungry, and both of us are guilty of moving the food around our plates more than we eat it at the kitchen table. The kitchen seems so empty without Gran here. We wash the dishes in companionable silence, side by side. I catch Sahara's eye and see she finally looks peaceful. She smiles back at me, telling me how safe she feels here at the farm. It reminds her of her own home, then a memory must emerge, and she looks sad again. I vow to fix things for her if I can.

Sahara and I decide to head to bed after watching a movie, the strain of the last few days has knocked us both a bit. One of the farm hands wives has made up a couple of adjoining guest rooms for us. Sahara gasps in undisguised delight when she sees the room set up for her, the chunky pine bed has a floral comforter and matching curtains adorn the window. It's definitely a chick room. It's such a refreshing change from the dingy motel rooms we've spent the past few nights in, and I assume its worlds apart from whatever hovel Jerry had her locked-up in. This room looks safe and comfortable. I remind her that I'm just next door if she needs anything then bid her goodnight and head to my own room. I'm pleased to see it's not a floral extravaganza, but a more masculine room. Plain white bedding, with a tartan throw to add a splash of color. It's a relaxing room and right now that's exactly what I need.

I toss and turn for the first few hours, distracted by the knowledge that she's in the next room, and the inappropriate thoughts that accompany that realization. I've got to stop thinking of her in that way, I'm not the kind of guy who'd take advantage of a woman in her position. It's a shame my cock doesn't know that. I finally drift off and my dreams are full of her.

11

Cam

Pushing away the breakfast pots in front of me, I'm about to stand and take them to Sahara. I make the mistake of looking at her halfway through rising from my seat. Fuck. I sit down suddenly. She looks so hot wearing just my borrowed shirt. The early morning sun is blazing through the kitchen window, silhouetting her figure through the crisp white cotton, leaving nothing to the imagination.

The curve of her hips below her tiny waist, the perfect arch of her back; I'm silently praying that she doesn't turn around. It's almost as though she can hear my unspoken thoughts. She turns, and I almost lose it. The sun highlighting the swell of her pert breasts, she's totally oblivious to the effect she's having on me. I can't act on it, she's fragile, not to mention she's under my protection. What kind of a shit would that make me.

"Cam?" The way she says my name makes me realize she's been trying to ask me something, which I've totally ignored, too busy trying to keep my erection under control.

"Sorry, was in a world of my own." I offer.

"I just asked if you wanted more coffee." She gestures to the empty mug in front of me.

I nod my head in assent before I realize that means she'll be moving next to me. I try and conjure up the most boring thing I can, anything to stop thinking of the body beneath the shirt. She moves next to me, leaning over the table, her long hair brushing against my cheek. I can feel the heat from her body, she's so close. Her leg catches against mine and I pull away involuntarily.

"I'm sorry," she apologizes, a look of regret on her face. I hate that I made her feel like that. She's been through so much shit in her life, especially recently. She needs to know that not all men just want to use her. But, God, do I want to use her right now.

Sahara

I'm not sure what's wrong with Cam this morning, he seems uncomfortable around me, almost skittish even. Maybe he's just tired of spending time with me, he's got his own life to lead after all, I must be a burden to him. Once we got to the farm he seemed to relax, it's like I saw a different side to him, a glimpse of the real Cam. He let down his armor and I thought he was starting to feel comfortable around me. We watched a cheesy movie and the sound of his laughter lifted my weary soul. For the first time in a long time I felt safe.

This morning it's like I'm sharing the house with a stranger. The way he flinched just now as I caught his leg left me feeling dirty. How can I expect any man to see me differently, I was Jerry's property after all? A chattel to be used and sold to the highest bidder.

I like Cam, it's not just that I feel safe with him. Under any other circumstances I'd probably have been attracted to him, there's a definite spark there. He'd never be interested in a girl like me though. Even I don't like me anymore so how could I expect anyone else to.

Unconsciously I shrink into myself, trying to make a smaller target, avoiding drawing attention. It doesn't work, Cam notices.

"Don't." His voice is gruffer than normal. "Don't put yourself down." I give him a quizzical look.

"I can see you change in front of me," he mutters. "You go from being you, happy, smiling, and brave to a shadow of you. Its like you're trying to hide from me."

"I'm sorry," I say again.

"Stop doing that!" Cam stands suddenly, his voice raised. I can't help it, I flinch. I'm rewarded with a look of pain crossing his face. He moves to me, grabbing hold of my shoulders so I'm forced to look him in the face. "Quit apologizing, you've done nothing to be sorry for." His hand reaches up and softly caresses my cheek. I lean into his touch, I can't remember the last time I was shown affection, and I like the feeling it gives me. "I'd never hurt you, Sahara, you have to believe that."

I do believe him. There's something about this man that I inherently trust. I've got to remember that he's my protector, nothing more, regardless of the effect his caress has on my body. Too soon his hands have released me, and I experience a profound sense of loneliness I can't explain. It's as though just that brief contact showed me the tantalizing promise of a future I can never have – the love and affection of a good man. That moment warmed my soul, before the cold reality of my life intruded.

I leave the jug of coffee on the table, and busy myself with carrying the dirty pots to the sink. I scrub them vigorously, long after they're clean. I need the distraction from my wayward thoughts. As tempting as a normal life is, I have to accept that girls like me don't get the dream. I have to just make the best of the shitty hand that life has dealt me.

I sense the heat of Cam's body behind me before I feel his arms cover mine, stopping the movement of the dish brush.

"I'm sorry," Cam breathes into my ear. "I can't help myself." Before I can begin to understand what he's apologizing for, I feel the touch of his lips on my neck. His kiss is light, gentle and sends a shiver down my spine.

He continues to kiss my neck as his hands move to my shoulders, then trace down my back until they rest on my hips, leaving a trail of heat in their wake. My traitorous body is responding, ignorant of the fact Cam deserves someone worthier than me. I can't and won't let him stop. I'm too greedy, too starved of affection for that.

He moves a step closer to me and I can feel the length of his erection pressing into my ass through the thin shirt. I want to reach back and touch him, but my hands remain gripped against the edge of the sink. If I let go I'll wake from this dream I'm sure. There's nothing dreamlike about the way his hands grab my ass, massaging firmly, before pulling me back towards him allowing his hard cock to grind against me. I'm so turned on right now just from a few touches, I'd probably spontaneously combust if he took it further.

His calloused fingers pinch my nipples through the cotton fabric, and I arch my back against him, exposing more of my neck to his greedy mouth. His teeth nip gently against my flesh and I can't help the moan of desire that escapes my lips.

No words are spoken as he turns me within the cage of his arms to face him, his mouth devouring mine. Our lips crash against each other as we kiss, greedily seeking out tongues, teeth nipping at lips. This isn't romance, this is carnal and my whole body is on fire. My heart is racing with the anticipation of where I want this to go.

Cam moves us to the kitchen table, turning me once again to face away from him. He guides my hands along the table-cloth till I'm leaning over it, the shirt lifting to reveal my naked ass to him. My breathing is so loud I can barely hear the clasp of the belt buckle being released, or the slow torturous descent of the zipper beneath. I do however feel the hardness of his cock as it's released from the confines of his jeans.

One hand pushes down on my lower back, keeping me in position whilst the other deftly torments my clit. I want to cry out loud with pleasure but am aware enough of my surroundings to remember the farm hands outside. My body is taught with pleasure. I'm close to breaking point as his fingers delve in and out of my wetness, teasing and tormenting me. I can't help it and call out, begging for release. Cam rewards me by pushing his cock deep inside my greedy pussy. The force of each movement crushing me against the table edge.

Cams hands move to grip my hips, pulling me back on his erection in time with each thrust. There's no gentleness here, just good old-fashioned fucking, and I love it! His hips move in circular movements creating a myriad of sensations for me; his cock pushing harder and faster into me each time. I feel the bliss of my orgasm just moments before Cam grunts his own, each pulse of his release accompanied by the glorious sound of his pleasure. That sound gives me so much satisfaction.

Cam lowers his chest against my back, I can feel his racing heartbeat and the heat of his skin against mine. As his breathing slows he caresses my neck, brushing my hair aside so he can plant gentle kisses against the back of my neck. In this instant everything feels right, for the first time in forever I feel at peace.

The moment doesn't last. It's as though Cam comes to his senses once his breathing is back under control and he pulls out suddenly.

"Oh shit, what have I done?" he cries, then rushes from the room. He's left me draped over the table, the evidence of his release creating a sticky trail down my thighs. I've never felt so humiliated in my life, not even by Jerry and that's saying something.

Drawing myself up I wrap my arms tightly around my chest, begging the tears not to fall.

"What did you expect?" I chastise myself as I leave the room, desperate for the sanctuary of the guest room I'm in. "What did you expect." I repeat. "You're just a worthless slut after all."

12

Declan

The hospital room is closing in on me. I can hear the low hiss of the oxygen flow that's breathing life into Gran. The rise and fall of her chest are barely visible, but the wheeze from the pneumonia sounds louder although it could just be my imagination.

My backside feels like it's gone numb in the hospital chair, as padded as it is. I guess it's to encourage visitors to go home. It's been a long day, Holly kept me company for a while, but this is no place for her, so I sent her back to the hotel.

The Docs are being cautious in what they tell me, I guess they don't want to get my hopes up or make promises they can't keep. Gran hasn't woken up yet, so they can't fully tell the extent of the stroke, although they're confident they got to her early enough to administer whatever special medication is supposed to help. They have told me that she's also got pneumonia and they seem to be more concerned with that than the stroke at the moment. I can hear the rattle in her lungs as her body fights for oxygen. She's attached to an antibiotic drip and looks so much smaller than I remember her. She never used to look this fragile. I shouldn't have left her. I should have stayed with her and taken care of her, repaid the love she showed me in my youth.

It doesn't seem to matter what I do since I left the army, everything is going wrong. Guilt seems to find some way to kick my ass every day. It rears its ugly head and reminds me of the failure I've made of my life and the mistakes I've made.

I look at my watch, but it's gone flat, it needs charging every night. I love Apple products, but their battery life leaves a lot to be desired. Hospital rooms are timeless, the nurses may do their rounds every few hours but other than that you have no way of knowing what time of day it is, and often even what day it is, although there's a slower pace on a weekend. I can hear birdsong outside the window so I'm guessing its around five am. Part of me wants to take comfort from the heralding of a new day, whilst part of me wants to just wring the frigging bird round the neck to shut up its cheerful melody. There's nothing to be cheerful about right now, not until Gran wakes up and I know she's going to be okay.

I shift in the seat, trying in vain to get comfortable, and rest my head on the side of the bed. I'm holding Gran's hand and talking to her about all sorts of nonsense from my child-hood. The nurse told me that even though she's uncon-scious she can hear me, and I should keep talking to her.

"Come on, Gran. Come back to me, you never sleep in this

late!" I admonish her, not too harshly though. She'd have been up already back on the farm, cooking breakfast for the guys before they headed off to work on the farm. I don't think I have a single memory of her being ill, or even having a lie in. She's always been the strong one, even when Grandpa died. She just got up each morning and carried on as normal.

"You'll never believe the scrape our Cam has got himself in..." I start to tell her. She adores Cam, and the feeling's mutual. I pause, unsure of what to say. If she can hear me then she'll only start to worry about him, and right now she needs to concentrate on healing and getting well again. Her hand is cold beneath mine as I gently rub my fingers over hers, wanting her to know that she's not alone, I'm with her. There's an almost imperceptible movement when I stop talking. I wonder if it's her way of telling me to continue? I'm not sure, but I continue to tell her about the last couple of days, deciding it can't make things any worse. Gran always encouraged me to talk my problems through with her. She rarely offered an opinion, believing that airing my problems out loud helped me focus on a solution. It doesn't help this morning, I'm still none the wiser on how we can get out of this mess. We just need to hope that Jack Snr comes on board and chooses us over his nephew. I'm pretty sure he will. If he doesn't we're in a pretty bad place. I'm so glad that I sent Gran a text with the burner phone number on, but I'm feeling guilty that I didn't take the time to ring her with it instead. I guess if I hadn't sent that text though, I would never have known she was ill, and Fred wouldn't have been able to get hold of me. Regret seems to be a constant state with me these days.

The door creaks open and one of the nursing assistants

comes in with her blood pressure machine. It must be time to check her stats again, it only feels like moments ago since they checked her. Maybe I did manage to nod off after all. The nurse advises me her temperature is still high, but that's to be expected until the antibiotics start to kick in, and her oxygen levels are stable thanks to the cannula in her nose. The whole time she's in the room she's talking to Gran, explaining what she's doing and just generally being chatty with her. It's different to the last nurse who came in, she worked in an uncomfortable silence that made me worry something was wrong. I guess in hindsight it was probably just near the end of a long shift for her and she wasn't feeling sociable.

As she leaves the room she offers me a drink; she's not supposed to, visitors are expected to fend for themselves down in the hospital coffee shop. I guess she's taken pity on me having been here all night. I decline. She suggests that I go freshen up at the hotel for an hour or two, Gran's stable and not showing any signs of waking up just yet. I'm torn between not wanting to leave her, and what she'd say if she woke up and saw me looking so disheveled. I can almost hear her displeasure in my head so agree to go grab a shower and change of clothes.

The hotel room is in darkness when I enter, and I stumble towards the bed, reluctant to turn on a light and wake Holly. I'm grateful for the lack of light after the over bright hospital environment. I undress down to my boxers and place my watch on the charging stand Holly has set up on the bedside table for me. I ease myself under the duvet and reach for her. Even in her sleep she senses my arrival and spoons into me, the warmth of her skin touching mine relaxing me. I wrap her in my arms and close my eyes for a moment, relishing the smell of her freshly washed hair. She feels like home, with her by my side I'm having fewer nightmares. I'm going to get some more counseling, it's the least I can do for her, and I need to know that I'm not going to hurt her in my sleep again. I can't risk it. Exhaustion creeps up on me and I enjoy a rare dreamless night, or rather what's left of it.

I'm woken by a gentle touch. Holly is sitting cross legged on the bed beside me, tracing a finger lightly along my abs, a huge grin on her face. "Morning, lover," she greets me.

"Morning to you too, beautiful," I respond, pulling her down into my arms and kissing her as though I haven't seen her for days. We chat a little about Gran, not that I really have anything to tell her that she hadn't already heard last night. I know I need to get back to the hospital, but I can't resist Holly's charms. "I've got to get back to Gran," I tell her, "but I need to grab a shower first, want to join me?" Her face lights up at my invitation.

"Of course I do dirty boy," she chuckles. "Besides, it would be rude not to!" She drags me to the ensuite and for the next half hour all I think about is Holly and just how fucking sexy she is, and how lucky I am that she's mine.

13

Sahara

I can't stop the tears from falling. Humiliated doesn't even begin to describe how I feel, but it's my own fault. I shouldn't have let it happen. I'm just a worthless slut after all. I don't deserve to be happy.

I was beginning to trust Cam, and I'd been trying to ignore the attraction I feel for him. That trust is destroyed now. I never imagined he could hurt me so cruelly. Sex with Cam was amazing, not that I have much experience of it, despite the way he found me.

Once again, the turn of a card has given me a moment beyond belief, followed by a betrayal I'm not sure I can come back from. My mind drifts back almost three years, to a time of innocence, happiness and security. Then a card turned and it all changed.

The sky out here is pitch black, but so clear the stars sparkle like crystals in the night. There's a bit of a chill, but the flickering flames of the campfire are doing a great job of keeping it at bay. Most of the gang have been drinking, although I've stuck with diet soda. My parents won't allow me to drink alcohol. They're very spiritual, very strict, and assure me that alcohol consumption will send me to the fiery pits of hell.

I'm amazed that I've been allowed to attend this camp out, but perhaps it's because I wasn't tempted to correct their assumption that this was a supervised trip. It's just a small group of us who are graduating and heading off to college at the end of summer. No teachers, and not as large a group as my parents believed. I am staying in a girls only tent though, I'm not capable of straying that far off the path they've laid out for me.

Some of the guys are starting to look a little out of it, not quite drunk, but not far from it. They've pulled out a pack of cards and are playing higher or lower for dares. Stupidly I agree to take part, and am playing against Tom, the guy I've been dating for a few months now. He offers me the pack and I groan as I draw a seven. He turns the card over that he's selected, and I can see straightaway it's a picture card. He gives me a look of apology as his friend Chas shouts with glee. "I've got this one! Sarah, I dare you to spend the night with Tom." The rest of the group dissolves into laughter. They've been taking the proverbial out of me for weeks because Tom and I haven't exchanged anything more than a few chaste kisses.

I'm too much my parent's daughter, I've been brought up to think that sex is something special that you save and share with 'the one'. I'm not naive, I know I'm probably the only virgin sitting round this fire, but I'm fine with that.

"Okay," I agree to Chas's challenge. The laughter dies on his lips, he's shocked by my acceptance. I trust Tom. I'll be fine.

Chas passes me another diet soda from the cooler and clinks his beer bottle to mine. "I didn't think you had it in you, Sarah." He salutes me with his beer.

Shortly after, the group splits and everyone heads back to their respective tents. My sleeping partner has decided she's going to share with Chas, so I can invite Tom into our tent. My head feels light and my movements aren't coordinated. I guess it must just be nerves. Did Chas put something in my drink? Surely, he wouldn't have done that, but it didn't taste quite the same as usual. Shaking the idea out of my head I change into my pj's and wait for Tom to arrive.

Tom stumbles as he enters the tent and I can tell he's been drinking. He apologizes for disturbing me, and for letting Chas put me in this position. "That's okay," I smile up at him, "I know I'm safe with you."

Tom gets a pained expression on his face which he quickly hides. "I wish you weren't," he says ruefully. I know Tom wants us to be more intimate, but I also know he respects that it's not something I'm ready for yet. "Can we at least cuddle?" He looks so forlorn that I can't help but agree.

Whatever is flowing through my system definitely has an effect on me, as does the sight of Tom in nothing but his boxers. In no time at all we're kissing more passionately than ever, and for the first time it's not enough for me. Tom is pushier and. more insistent than usual, his hands are exploring areas they've never ventured to before, and his kisses are demanding.

My body responds naturally, and the longer we embrace the

more I want. I'm so engrossed by Tom and his skillful hands that the last thing I think of is my parents, and the celibacy they expect of me. Primal urges take over, and before I know it I'm no longer a virgin. It was clumsy and uncoordinated, and nothing at all like the sentimental experience I'd expected. It was also quicker than I'd thought, and as I'd hoped for stars and an afterglow of orgasmic bliss, I was definitely a little disappointed. Tom seemed to enjoy it, although he fell asleep on top of me as soon as he'd finished.

Sex with Cam had been nothing like that first time with Tom. It had been wild and primal and was amazing. Sex with Tom had been very vanilla and hadn't lived up to expectations.

More tears fall as I remember the last time I saw Tom, hooked up to life support and looking like a shadow of himself, right before his mother ordered me out of the room and out of his life.

Tom and I didn't sleep together again, although we'd had some pretty serious foreplay over the following months. We'd become so close and decided to room together at college. I never met his parents, but I somehow understood that they wouldn't approve. Tom came from a lot of wealth and with that came responsibilities, an expectation that he would marry within his own class and enter the political arena, his fathers failed ambition for his own life.

It took me two weeks to pluck up the courage to tell him I was pregnant, two weeks of hiding in the bathroom looking at that little blue line and wondering how something so small and insignificant as that dash of color could turn my whole life upside down.

I remember the day he proposed so clearly. I'd expected him to run for the hills at my news, instead he dropped to his knees, kissed my belly and asked me to marry him. For one whole afternoon I was the happiest I've ever been. It was like something out of one of those Hallmark movies I loved.

Then fate decided that I wasn't allowed to be happy. It was hours before I heard the news, officially I wasn't part of Tom's life, so no one had deemed it important that I be told. In the end it was Chas who called me. There'd been an accident, I knew Tom had been on the way to tell his parents our news, and he'd insisted on going on his motorbike. He loved that thing. A truck driver had run a red light, after an afternoon of drinking. Tom's small Honda hadn't stood a chance against the size and power of the speeding truck.

When I finally made it to the hospital the news was grim. Tom was in a coma, he'd suffered a massive brain injury, and they weren't sure he'd survive the night. I sat at his side, holding his hand and telling him how much I loved him and our baby. That was the moment his mother walked in and banished me. I've never seen so much hatred on another human being's face. She'd obviously been spying on me and listening in to my conversation.

"If you think for one moment you're going to pass off your white trash bastard as my sons' child you've got another thing coming!" She practically spat the words at me as I cowered back in my chair, my hand protectively cradling the bump that was only just starting to show. "There's no way my son would lower himself to sleep with someone like you," she sneered. "Now get out, and if I ever see you again I'll have security escort your cheap ass out of the hospital and press charges." I sat frozen, unable to comprehend how someone so vile could have given birth to someone as pure and good and loving as Tom. "Did you hear me?" She shrieked as she pointed her perfectly manicured hand at the door. I stumbled as I rose from my position at the side of the bed, silent tears streaming down my face.

"I love you, Tom," I whispered into his hair as I placed what I knew would be my last kiss on his forehead. Shielding my bump, I rose and held my head high.

Regardless of what this woman thought, Tom had loved me, and he'd wanted our baby. I didn't want to go on without him, but I would. Our baby needed me to be strong.

That was the day that my life started its descent into darkness and spiraled out of control. That was the day that started me on the path to the worthless whore I've become.

One by one I've had to put my hopes and dreams aside, until now I'm left with none. I've had to grow up and realize that life is never going to be like that for me. I just have to get on with it.

Call me stupid, despite everything I've been through I'm still the little girl who wants to believe in a fairytale ending. I want to believe that I'm the best thing that ever happened to someone.

More tears fall, and I'm no longer sure whether I'm crying for Tom, the baby that I've lost, the way Cam treated me, or if it's just self-pity. Regardless of the reason, the tears continue to fall.

14

Declan

I close the door of Gran's hospital room as gently as I can. Even at this late hour there's activity. The lights may have been dimmed, and most patients asleep, but there's the low murmur of the night staff's voices as they make their way around the beds, constantly checking on those in their care. The monotonous beep beep of monitors accompanies it all. I leave the ward as quietly as possible, conscious that I don't want to disturb this fragile peace that surrounds everything.

It's been a tough day, Gran still hasn't woken up. I've sat and talked to her and held her hand in mine. It's like talking to a stranger. The woman in the bed doesn't look like Gran, she's fragile and seems so small beneath the sheets. My Gran is an indomitable force, she's the strongest woman I know. These two women, although the same person, seem poles apart from each other. It's almost feels like I'm in the room of someone I don't know.

The lift doors open to an empty lobby, aside from a sole security guard on the desk. It's a massive contrast to the busy hustle during the day where you can't move for the sea of bodies filling the area. Free of the lift I take out my phone to check in with Cam.

From the moment he answers I can tell somethings not right, his voice doesn't hold its normal vitality. We chat about the farm, the day to day running of it is being handled by the foreman, but Cam's keeping an eye out. He's hired a temporary housekeeper as the farm hands are used to Gran cooking all their meals. There doesn't seem to be any sign of Jerry or his hired goons yet which is good, hopefully hiding Sahara at the farm is working. It's when we're talking about Sahara that his voice really changes.

"What's wrong, Cam?" I ask. "Has something happened with Sahara?" I know she sent a text cancelling her shopping trip with Holly this morning, but thought she just had a headache

"I fucked up, Declan." I can hear Cam's sigh down the phone line. "I fucked her." The defeat in his voice is something I'm not used to hearing. I know he's a bit of a lad when it comes to the ladies, but I hadn't expected him to sleep with Sahara. Don't get me wrong, she's attractive, but she's under our protection which makes her a no go, or so I'd thought.

"What the hell?" I splutter out, the shock of what he told me overriding my usual sensitivity.

"It was a spur of the moment thing." He really sounds

dejected. "It was amazing. I couldn't help myself and she was in to it just as much as me, but it shouldn't have happened, and I may have let her know that a little too brutally." He sighs again. "She's not talking to me, she won't even come out of her room."

"I don't know what to say Cam, this isn't like you." I'm not the best person to be giving advice on this kind of thing. My relationship with Holly is still new, and I'm not the same person I was when I was last involved with anyone seriously. "Do you like her that way?"

"Yeah, I do, but I can't go there. I'm supposed to be protecting her, not fucking her over the kitchen table." He sounds so dejected.

"I hope you scrubbed it well," I laugh. "Gran would have your ass for that if she knew." I can just see Gran chasing Cam around the kitchen with a scrubbing brush.

"I'll get right on it!" Cam finally laughs. He knows Gran too well to know that's exactly what she'd do.

"Want me to get Holly to ring her, see how she's doing?" I offer.

"Yeah, that might help. Maybe after talking to Holly she'll let me apologize."

We agree to catch up again tomorrow, and I hang up the phone as I arrive outside the hotel room door.

Holly is fast asleep when I enter the room. I shower quickly and crawl in beside her. The nurse had assured me Gran wouldn't wake up tonight, and if anything happened they'd call me. I'm careful not to wake Holly. She's out for the count, although her body senses mine and she moves back into my embrace, allowing us to spoon. After today her touch is exactly what I need, reassuring me that I'm not alone in all of this. Sleep quickly claims me and I enjoy a night without nightmares.

※

"**H**ey, lover," Holly greets me as I wake. She's sitting astride me, her fingers drawing a lazy trail across my chest as I slowly come around. She leans forward, her lips grazing mine in greeting. At this angle I have a perfect view of her breasts as they threaten to fall out of the tiny vest she slept in. Pushing aside the material I greedily draw a nipple into my mouth, lightly catching it between my teeth. My girl moans, causing my already hard erection to push against her knickers. I can feel her desire through them. I reach up, palming her heavy breasts in my hands, before tweaking her other nipple in my fingers. Holly throws her head back in delight and grinds herself into my crotch. Her sudden movement pulls her breasts out of reach of my mouth and I pout in displeasure.

"Don't worry, you'll have them back soon enough," she laughs. "But first...". Holly slowly moves down my body, kissing, nipping and biting as she goes. When she reaches my boxers, she stops. "These need to go." Mere seconds are all the time it takes for her to free my erection and resume her position astride me. Her hand delicately traces the length of my cock, before her fingers clasp around it. Her firm grip moves up and down my length. It feels amazing, but not as amazing as when she lets go and her tongue takes over. Her hot mouth quickly replaces her tongue and I'm not sure how much longer I can last. Holly must sense it and releases me. "As much as I'd love you to come in my mouth, I need to feel you." She discards her knickers and positions herself above my cock. She doesn't take it slowly, instead she takes me in one quick movement, then pauses, my cock seated balls deep in her.

When she starts to move it's slow at first, pulling her vest top over her head she tosses it aside then leans forward, her hair soft against my chest as she brings her breasts close enough for me to reach with my mouth again. I'm flicking my tongue against her hard nipples when she pulls back suddenly, her back straightening as she takes my full length deep inside her again.

"Fuck, I love how deep you are when I sit back," She smirks. Maintaining the position, she increases her pace. Her head is thrown back in ecstasy now, her moans of pleasure making me harder than I thought possible. As much as I want to delay my release and enjoy this moment, the feel of her hot, tight pussy at this angle is my undoing. We come together, Holly collapsing on top of me. We're both a hot sweaty mess, but I'm pretty sure the look of bliss on her face is reflected in mine.

"I think you need a shower, dirty boy," she grins at me.

"Well, it would be rude not to!" I reply.

Even with another hot encounter in the shower I'm able to make it back to the hospital before Gran shows any signs of waking up.

15

Cam

Sahara is finally sitting across the table from me, holding onto her coffee mug as though her life depends on it. At least she's left her room today, so I guess that's progress. She won't look me in the eye though. She replied quietly when I wished her a good morning as she walked in, but there was none of the warmth in her voice I'd become used to. It's my fault, and I'm not sure how to fix it. The smile has gone from her eyes. I did that. At least she's wearing clothes today, I don't think I could handle seeing her in nothing more than my shirt again. I don't think I'll ever be able to wipe that image from my mind.

"I'm sorry, Sahara." She looks up at me finally, her eyes still guarded. "The other morning was a mistake." Wrong choice of word, she visibly flinches when I say it. I'm no good at this emotional crap, I'm a love them and leave them kind of guy. "What I mean is, well, I shouldn't have." From the expression on her face I'm still not saying the right thing.

"You deserve better than this," I try and tell her. I'm trying to get across that she's too good for me, that I'm supposed to be looking out for her and I've broken that trust. It's not coming out that way and the look of hurt on her face is killing me. Before I can come up with the wrong words again she interrupts me.

"Really?" She sounds surprised. "I don't deserve shit. I've lost everything I ever cared about, everyone I ever cared about. My parents, my boyfriend, my baby." She's back to the flat, emotionless Sahara I first met and it's my fault. I've fucked up. I barely register the word baby, she's never mentioned that before, I make a mental note to add that to the list of things we need to talk about, but right now I need to fix what's wrong between us.

"I'm..." before I can get the apology out Sahara stops me.

"Don't." She places her coffee cup calmly on the table, but I can see she's so angry that she's shaking. "I was stupid to think it meant anything. I should know by now that I'll never be good enough for anything other than a quick fuck, but I've not quite learned that lesson yet. You hurt me when you rejected me like that. You made me feel like the cheap piece of ass that I've become. There was just enough of the old me left that for that small moment of time I felt like someone wanted me, that I was special, that I wasn't all alone. I'm sorry I was so naive." She stands from the table, still shaking, yet her voice is full of calm determination.

"If you'll excuse me, I'm not strong enough right now to put on a brave face. I'm sure you're a good guy, Cam, and genuinely sorry, but now every time I see you it's going to be a reminder that I wasn't good enough, I'll never be good enough." She picks up her coffee cup and refills it at the counter, before leaving the kitchen, her final words cutting me deeply. "You made me feel like a cheap whore."

I sink back down to the table, not sure how I came to be standing. I must have risen at the same time she did, ingrained manners drilled into me by my Mama. She'd whup my ass for the way I've acted. I've fucked up, and I've no idea how to fix this. The last thing I wanted was to hurt Sahara. I've never treated a woman like a whore, it's not me, but I'm not a relationship kind of guy. I just couldn't help myself. I've been drawn to Sahara since I first met her, despite my unwritten rule never to mix business with plea-sure. Sahara deserves better than me, she needs a guy who'll romance her and want a future with her, someone who'll cherish her and love her. That guy sure as hell isn't me. 'If you're looking for romance, you're in the wrong house' has always been my mantra.

Bits of the conversation torment me, what did she mean by she'd lost everyone, and what did she mean she'd lost her baby. She doesn't look old enough to be a mother. She doesn't look old enough to have suffered so much loss. Now I've fucked up, I'm pretty sure she won't share her story with me. I want nothing more than to make things right for her, to put a smile back on her face. All I've done is make things worse. I don't understand life, how it can deal one person such a shitty hand, especially someone so young. I've seen stuff that can't be unseen, unspeakable horrors that will haunt me forever. There's nothing I can do about those. I will make things right for Sahara though, I have to.

I pick up the phone to Holly, grateful for Declan's offer, and hope to hell she can fix this cluster fuck I've created.

Holly pulls no punches when she answers the phone, I guess Declan already filled her in.

"What the fuck, Cam!" Holly shouts at me through the handset. "How could you?" I can hear the disappointment in her voice.

"I messed up, Holly," I admit. "Can you help me fix this?" I tell Holly everything, how I've fought my attraction to Sahara since the night I met her, how I couldn't help myself yesterday, and how I fucked up again today. Holly gasps when I tell her what Sahara said about the baby.

"How?" Holly asks. I admit I don't know, and after the way I've treated Sahara there's no way she's going to open up to me now. "Bring her to the city," she suggests. "I'm guessing we still need to get her some clothes and shit, but I don't want to leave Declan right now. He needs me. I'll take her shopping and see if I can get her to open up to me, you can be there for Declan at the hospital." I agree, that's if I can persuade Sahara to even talk to me now. We never did get to the mall after our disastrous hook up, so it's as good an excuse as any.

I ask Holly how Declan's Gran is doing, he's seemed pretty positive on the phone to me, but maybe too positive. "I over-heard the nurses talking amongst themselves," she confesses. "I don't think Declan realizes how serious it is. I think it's just a question of when, not if." She hasn't told him what she heard as she's desperately hoping they were wrong. I think we both know in our gut that they weren't.

The pneumonia seems to be on the mend, but the stroke looks to have been too serious to come back from.

I agree to call Holly back once I've spoken to Sahara. I need to get the two of them together, so Holly can fix my mess, and it looks like I need to go say goodbye to an amazing old lady and be there for my friend. What was I saying about life being cruel? I'm struggling with the thought of losing Gran myself, and I'm scared of what that loss will do to Declan.

I head upstairs, determined but devastated.

16

Cam

*T*he drive to the hospital is hard, and aside from the music playing at low volume, it's in silence. Sahara refuses to even look at me, never mind talk to me. The scenery is failing to distract me, normally I find it soothing. I love spending time at the farm, but I'm too disturbed by the colossal fuck up I've made to take any comfort from it.

Sleeping with Sahara was a mistake in that it shouldn't have happened, but I don't regret the act itself, we fitted together so well. I want to tell her I was wrong, but I can't get the words out. If I'm honest with myself I want to sleep with her again, but I'm not a relationship kind of guy and she deserves better. I also feel a bit of a dick, I was supposed to be rescuing her, and here I am just taking advantage, at least that's how it feels.

Just thinking about Jerry and the plans he had for Sahara

make my blood boil. I smash my hand on the steering wheel, drawing her attention. I shrug my shoulders, and she resumes her silent staring through the passenger window. I don't think it's possible for her to be physically any further away from me right now, she's practically hugging the door frame, and her body language is clearly warning me off.

My sixth sense suddenly kicks in and tells me that something is wrong, outside of the car that is. I'm not that much of an idiot that I can't tell things are very wrong inside the vehicle. I feel my hackles rise which tells me I'm being watched, but there's nothing obvious. There's been very little traffic on the road around us, and none of that caused me any concern. The vehicles fit the surroundings, and the drivers blend in with the vehicles. Despite finding nothing obvious when I scan the area again I still have the feeling that something is wrong, someone is out there watching us.

My body has tensed, on the alert, but Sahara is ignorant of my concerns. She continues to stare out of the window. I'm not sure how much she's actually taking in of what we're passing, but I suspect it's not a lot. I get the feeling she's lost in her own little world again. She seems to spend a lot of her time there, and I'm concerned that it's not a good place for her to be. I feel the need to comfort her, but right now I'm sure I'm the last person she wants to be around. I want to reassure her that she's safe now, but until we know what Jerry has planned, I can't. I just hope that when we get to the hospital, Holly can offer her a shoulder to cry on.

We arrive at the hospital without incident, but my sixth sense still tells me to be on the alert. No vehicles have followed us into the parking lot, nor seemed to follow us for long enough to have been a tail. I just can't shake the feeling that something isn't right, but with no evidence to back it up I need to accept it's just my imagination.

I have to reach over and get Sahara's attention once I've taken the keys from the ignition. She's so lost to her thoughts she jumps as my hand touches her. I jerk my arm back, and instantly apologize for startling her. Her grey eyes are so dark as she stares back at me, there's no emotion there. It's as though she's gone back to being the girl I rescued the other night, she's numb and distant from me again.

As she steps down from the truck I reach into the glovebox, pulling out the handgun I'd hidden there earlier and hide it in the back of my jeans. I know I shouldn't be carrying it in public, but there's no way I'm going anywhere without it until that sixth sense calms down and stops leaving me feeling like I'm going to be ambushed any moment.

Sahara is a few steps ahead of me when a small toddler rushes out into the car park, oblivious of any traffic that may be around and barrels straight into her, knocking them both to the floor. His harried mother finally catches up to them just as I reach Sahara's side. She's risen to a seated position and is holding the little boy close to her, protective arms around his tiny frame. She's murmuring words into his ear so quietly I can't hear her, but he has stopped the wailing that had started as soon as he hit the ground. His mother snatches him from Sahara, almost smothering him as she alternates between thanking Sahara and telling the child off for running away from her. She's admonishing him at the same time she's planting kisses all over his face. Yeah, I think that kid's really going to get the message, not. I can see how she'd be relieved though, he ran straight out into a busy car park and could have been killed.

I watch the mother carry the child away to a parked car, before I realize I haven't checked if Sahara was hurt in the tumble. When I look at her I'm surprised to see fat, heavy tears rolling down her face and she's looking longingly after the child. What on earth?

"Are you hurt?" I ask her, bending to check her over for injuries before I try and help her stand. She shakes her head violently. Her tears are heavier now and she's starting to make an awful wailing noise.

"Sophia!" She cries out, then doubles over, sobbing uncontrollably. I'm lost. I've no idea how to deal with a woman who's only crying a little, so this hysteria is well out of my comfort zone.

I awkwardly try and pat her on the back, but she pulls away from me, still out of control. I try to persuade her to move to one of the benches at the perimeter of the car park, but she's having none of it. If I'm not careful someone's going to come barreling into the car park and wipe her out. As usual, when I don't know what to do I pick up the phone and ask Declan for help.

I t feels like forever before Holly appears through the hospital doors, although I'm sure in reality it was only moments. I'm getting odd looks from passersby, as Sahara is still sobbing uncontrollably. She's gasping for breath and wailing the name Sophia at the same time. I've no idea who Sophia is, she's never mentioned her before.

"What the hell?" Holly looks at me accusingly as she rushes over to embrace Sahara. I'm already in the shit with her, and this can only have made it worse.

"Shh, honey," she soothes. "I'm here for you now. Its Holly," she croons. Sahara doesn't hear her at first, so Holly repeats herself until she finally has her attention. Holly helps Sahara to stand, leading her over to one of the benches, where she sits her down and draws her into her arms. Sahara rests her head over Holly's legs as Holly gently strokes her hair and keeps offering soothing words. The violent shaking has slowed down now, and the gasping sobs are less frequent.

Holly looks over at me accusingly and I just shrug my shoulders in return. It wasn't my fault this time, I'm not sure what the hell caused it. She was fine until the toddler knocked into her.

Once Sahara finally calms down to where she's just crying, Holly tries to do a quick once over to check for injuries.

"Sahara, honey, are you hurt?" She questions her.

Sahara stutters out a negative response, still not capable of stringing proper words together. The girls sit there for a little, while I stand there looking like a spare part and feeling just as useless.

Eventually Sahara calms down enough for Holly to persuade her into the ladies' room so she can clean up her face. Holly tells me that they're going to get a coffee in the coffee shop, and that I should go and visit with Declan and his Gran.

"I'll take care of Sahara," Holly offers. "I think Declan could do with a friendly face right now." I can see the concern in Holly's face, and guess I'm not going to be walking into good news.

Can today get any worse? I have a horrible feeling that it can.

17

Sahara

When I saw that little boy running towards me in the car park and then held him in my arms the pain was indescribable. He's the same age that my daughter Sophia would be. My arms yearn to hold her again, to nuzzle her baby soft hair, to hear the light musicality of her giggle as she found something new to entrance her.

It's not to be. I'm never going to be able to feel those things again. All I'm left with is memories, and some of those are fading. I'm scared that soon I'll have nothing left to remember her by. I can't recall her smell anymore, it was a mix of baby powder and soap, but it eludes me now. Her voice is hard to recall now as well, but when I close my eyes I see her smile, the look of joy she would throw my way when I entered a room and she glimpsed me.

I wonder, often, what I did wrong to deserve a life that held so much promise but was all rudely taken away from me. I loved my parents, did my chores, did well at school, I was the perfect daughter, right up to the point I turned that playing card and they turned their backs on me. How can a religion that preaches love condone turning your back on your own child? I may have only had Sophia for a few short years, far too few, but there is nothing I wouldn't have done for my daughter.

The first time I held her in my arms I was lost to her. I looked into those dark baby eyes of hers and knew right then that she was a part of my heart. As scared as I was, having had to go through it all on my own, and knowing that the future meant more of the same, I knew I could handle anything for her. She was worth it.

And now I'm alone, seeing that little boy was a painful and stark reminder of that. The way his mother snatched him from my arms you'd have thought I was trying to hurt him, not protect him.

Holly has arrived, and I have to wonder what I've said or done over the last few minutes. Did I reveal my secret? What did I say? The look on Cam's face is one of anguish, and fear. What have I done or said that's caused him to look at me like that? Holly looks scared as well. I was so lost in my grief I don't know what just happened.

Holly is on the bench with me, holding me in a hug so tight I think she's scared I'll try and run away. I almost laugh, right now I'm not even sure I have the strength to stand let alone run. When she suggests we go get a coffee I think I nod my head in agreement. She helps me to get up and I stand there on shaky legs, hoping they'll keep me upright. What I really want to do is go find somewhere dark and just lie down and quit on life. I feel so hollow. The other morning with Cam I felt more alive than I have in forever, but then he told me it was all a mistake and destroyed what little hope I had left in life. I have a feeling that Holly isn't going to let me get away with hiding away, so I follow her meekly to the bathroom when she tells me I need to freshen up. Yeah, Holly, a splash of cold water on my face is going to fix everything! I really need to get hold of the sarcasm running through my mind before I say something out loud that I'll regret. These people haven't done anything to hurt me, apart from Cam, but deep down I know his intention is to keep me safe from harm. Still, I just want to go to sleep and not wake up any more. I'm not brave enough to end things, I just don't want to wake up. I want the decision taken away from me, I want that calm nothingness that only exists in sleep.

The dull hospital walls are a grim reminder of the last time I saw Tom. Memories assault me, even down to my reflection in the bathroom mirror as I wipe the tear tracks from my face. I'd run to the bathroom after my encounter with his mother and wiped away my tears. No idea then of the hell that was to continue to unleash itself on my life. I'm not sure why those memories are the ones I hold of hospitals when the happiest day of my life should be the overriding one. Perhaps it's my minds way of keeping me sane. I can't think of Sophia, not now, I can't handle that pain at the moment.

Holly is chattering away at me and I realize I haven't heard a word she has been saying.

"You didn't hear a word I just said, did you?" She's intuitive, I'll give her that. I just shake my head in response, my throat feels raw from all the crying and I'm not sure I could get any words out if I tried. She gives me such a look of warmth in response, then draws me into a hug. That's dangerous territory for me, hugs mean someone cares, and I can't allow myself to be deceived by that. I'm on my own, I need to accept that and get on with what's left of my life...alone. I try to draw back, but she doesn't let me.

"I don't know what that was about, Sahara, but I get that you're not ready to talk about it." She finally releases me from the hug, stepping back and looking me square in the eye. "When you're ready to talk to me about it, I'll be here to listen," she offers. "Right now, you look like you could do with a strong coffee, come on."

I like this girl. She's strong and sassy, and in another life, I could see her being a friend. I don't want her to get hurt because of me, and if I stay around here I can see that happening. I need to find a way to leave, I don't think I could handle anyone else I care about getting hurt because of me.

Holly

Sahara has put the barriers up. I'm not sure what happened in the car park, but it was obviously a really painful memory for her. I get the feeling she wants to bolt, so I'm going to have to tread carefully with her. I'm not going to push her to tell me what's wrong, but I will find out. Seeing her in that much pain hurts me, and I could see it was upsetting Cam as well. We might not have known this girl for long, but we already care about her. That's why I'm so bloody angry with Cam for sleeping with her and messing it up.

From what little she has told us she's had a terrible few years, she was almost sold into the fucking sex trade. It makes my blood boil to think of this beautiful girl being treated like that, and the thought of what the future held for her before Cam rescued her just doesn't bear thinking about.

We're a similar age, and I don't know if I could handle what she's been through. Then I realize that I've lived through my own hell, we're both stronger than we know. I just need to help her find herself again.

18

Unknown

*T*he scene in the hospital car park was interesting to watch as it unfolded. The way the big guy was looking around it was as though he could sense my presence, but I'm too good at my job. He doesn't know I'm here watching him. I need to be alert around him, something tells me he's no ordinary civilian.

The girl that I'm looking for is there, right in front of me. She's a wreck which makes her vulnerable. There's too much activity out here, I just need to get her on her own then take her back to Jerry. I don't know what he wants her for, but I can guess. I've heard the rumors, but as long as I'm getting paid I don't let morals get in the way of the job. I'm not one of Jerry's goons, he's a nobody with an overinflated ego, instead I choose to work for the highest bidder. The bounty on this job isn't that great, but I'm bored, and the challenge will give me something to fill my days before I decide on my next assignment.

The brunette that's with her looks pretty hot, I wouldn't mind tapping that. She's feisty, and I like it when they fight back. I palm my cock beneath my trousers, allowing myself to get a little excited over the things I'd like to do to her. Maybe I'll grab the both of them and keep the friend for my own entertainment.

My attention is drawn back to the little group in the car park, they're making a move, heading into the hospital out of sight. That's okay, I can wait. I'm a patient man.

Declan

When the hospital door opens behind me I look over expecting to see Holly. Instead its Cam who comes in. I stand, and we meet in an awkward hug. God I've missed my friend.

His face pales when he looks over and sees Gran in the hospital bed. This is the first time he's seen her in a few months. "Wow, Declan," he gulps. "That's the first time I've ever looked at your Gran and thought she looks old." There's sadness in his voice. Cam moves over to the chair on the far side of the bed and sits down, taking hold of Gran's hand as he does so. They've removed the drip and the canula now so at least she's not hooked up to machines. I'm not sure if that makes me feel any better, as part of me feels it's a sign that they're giving up on her.

"Hey, Gran," he croons as he strokes her hand. "It's me, Cam. Are you going to open your eyes for me?" he pleads with her. There's no change, no sign that she knows he's here even. It's been like this since the first night I arrived. I kid myself on occasion that she has responded to something I've said, but it's just wishful thinking on my part.

The Doctor has not long left and he told me to prepare for the worst. Gran isn't responding to treatment. At this stage if she did wake up its pretty certain that there would be permanent disability and it's unlikely she would be able to care for herself. Gran would hate that. She's always been the strongest person that I know. I'm not sure what I'm going to do without her in my life. Although I moved away I always knew she was there for me, back on the farm, or on the other end of the phone. A shudder passes through me, I can't even begin to contemplate life without her. The woman practically raised me. Cam is chattering away to her, oblivious to the fact she's not responding, or is he? He's a bright guy and I am pretty sure he's realized what's happening.

Cam pauses his conversation to look over at me, the unspoken question in his eyes. I shake my head in response. A look of sadness passes over his face for a fleeting moment before he resumes his chat with Gran. He's updating her about the activity on the farm, how everything's going well and he's keeping an eye on it for her although the farm hands are complaining his cooking isn't up to Gran's standards. Even that comment gains no response. If anything would have done, that would have been it.

Now there are no wires or drips attached to Gran, you could almost believe she was sleeping if you didn't know any better. But I do. The knowledge is eating away at me. I haven't told Holly yet, but I think she knows. I'm hoping that if I don't say the words out loud then it can't be true. It's just wishful thinking on my part, and I should know better. Why Gran? She's always put everyone else first, been a god fearing and righteous woman her whole life. She doesn't deserve this. My only consolation is that she's not suffering, or so the nurses have reassured me.

Cam runs out of things to tell Gran, so we sit there in silence for a while, either side of her, each holding one of her hands, and praying for a miracle.

"I think we were followed here today," Cam eventually offers. "I couldn't see anyone, but I had that sixth sense." Cam was always spot on with his intuition out in Afghanistan, if he said something was off, we believed him. I groan that we now have Jerry to worry about on top of Gran. It's a distraction I could do without.

"Maybe I should take Sahara somewhere else," Cam suggests, reading my mind as he so often does.

"No!" I whisper loudly, not wanting to startle Gran although I'm pretty certain she can't hear me. "We'll call the guys, you can't do this on your own. We'll have your back." I pause. "I don't want to leave Gran while she's like this, but the farm is a good place to hole up. We've got plenty of eyes out there, and we know the lay of the land."

Cam shakes his head. "It's only a hunch so far, if anything happens then I'll call the guys. I'll get on to Chris and see when the gear is arriving. That should see us right," he offers. We'd had to leave the pickup full of weapons behind when we boarded the flight, so Chris had arranged for it to be driven over to us. It should be here any time. "You need to stay here and concentrate on your Gran." He's right, but I don't like him trying to handle this on his own. We work as a team, always have, and we promised when we came back from Afghanistan that we'd always have each other's backs. I guess him telling me to stay here with Gran is his way of covering me.

"It's so quiet in here." Cam looks around the clinical room. Hospital policy is no flowers, but the windowsill is covered in an array of colorful get-well cards from friends and well-wishers. "Would they let us play some music for your Gran?" he suggests. That's not a bad idea, Gran always has the radio on at home. She says it keeps her company when everyone is out on the farm. I'll ask the nurse when she does her next check. They did say I should keep talking to Gran as she can hear me, even if she can't respond, but like Cam, I've run out of ideas to chat with her about.

"I'll ask Holly to bring a CD player in with her," I suggest. That's when Cam tells me what happened outside in the car park. Holly has taken Sahara to the hospital coffee shop, I doubt she'll be up to the planned shopping trip from what he's told me. We're both saddened that someone so young could have suffered so much, but then I look over at the bed and realize that life is just a series of episodes we have to endure. We can only hope that some of those moments are good memories that will get us through the bad times ahead.

19

Cam

The afternoon in the hospital has drained me. I can't believe that's the same old lady that I know and love. I guess we're all hoping for a miracle, but deep down we know it's not going to happen. We just need to be there for Declan as this is going to hit him hard, especially after what he went through in Afghanistan and then losing Max when we got home.

The elevator descends slowly through each floor, stopping to admit a couple, she's sobbing into a handkerchief whilst the man, who I assume is her husband tries to console her. I try not to listen in on their whispered conversation but it's hard not to in this confined space. They are married, and her husband has just been told he has terminal cancer. Despite being the recipient of life changing news he's the one trying to offer support and consolation. It's both humbling and heartbreaking to watch. The lift doors open again admitting a young couple and a newborn baby. In this cramped metal box I'm surrounded by the extremities of life. It's also a stark reminder that whilst one family is hearing the worst news that another is celebrating the joy of new life. It's good to realize that hospitals are a place for celebration as well. The sight of the child reminds me that I need to find out what happened to Sahara's baby.

The coffee shop is quiet now that it's early evening and the girls are sitting in a corner near the window. They don't notice my approach, meaning Sahara startles in her seat when I move to sit down next to her. 'I'm sorry," I offer in apology. She nods her acceptance then moves back to fidgeting with her cup. Holly gives me a look of resigned defeat. It's obvious she's no nearer to finding out what caused the breakdown in the car park earlier. I'm surprised as I know how tenacious Holly can be, and I've been gone for several hours.

Holly offers to refresh their coffees and asks me what I would like. Placing my order, I hand her some cash to cover it. She's about to protest then changes her mind and heads over to the counter. I take a moment to scan the room, more from habit than anything and am concerned when my sixth sense kicks in. I don't see anything obvious or out of place so assume it's off kilter again.

Sahara looks at me and offers me a weak smile. "I'm sorry about earlier," she offers.

"It's okay, do you want to talk about it?" I try not to push too hard, I don't want to scare her off. She shakes her head.

"Not yet." It's progress of a kind I suppose. I've just got to be patient with her, let her know she can talk to me and that

I'll be there for her. It's not going to be easy after the way I treated her the other morning.

Holly returns with the coffees and some blueberry muffins. I remember Declan telling me their first date was coffee and blueberry muffins. It's a good memory to hold onto right now. Sahara nurses the warm cup and just toys at picking crumbs of muffin off and nibbling them. Holly shows no such finesse, taking great bites from hers and then giving me a guilty grin as I reach over to brush away a crumb from the side of her very full mouth.

"How is she today?" Holly asks, her muffin now devoured.

"No change I don't think." I pause, not wanting to say the words out loud for fear of making them a reality. "I don't think..." I can't continue.

"It's okay, Cam," Holly places a comforting hand on mine. "He knows, he just can't say it out loud yet." It's a reminder of how in tune Declan and I are. "It's just a question of when."

We spend a while chatting about Gran, I'm the only one of the three of us who knows her, and I share some of my happier memories with the girls. The mood around the table lightens a little when I tell a story about her chasing Declan from the kitchen with a frying pan once after he'd dared to tell her his egg wasn't runny enough at breakfast.

Holly yawns and looks at her watch. It's almost nine and I still have to drive back to the farm. I glance at the floor near Sahara and see an obvious lack of shopping bags. Holly notices and offers an apology. Sahara just wasn't in the right place for retail therapy this afternoon. Holly suggests we check in to the hotel for the night and she'll go pick up some clothes for her in the morning. It's not a bad idea, saves me a four hour round trip at least and I reassure Sahara that we'll get a twin room. I don't have to tell her that she's not staying on her own whilst Jerry is still out there.

I walk the girls to the truck and spot a piece of paper under the windscreen. Assuming it's just an advertising flyer I grab it and toss it on the dashboard, ignoring it for another time.

The check in at the hotel takes no time and soon we're settled into the room. Holly has lent Sahara something to sleep in thankfully, so I don't have to suffer the sight of her in my shirt again.

Sahara is still distant with me, although she answers positively when I ask her if she wants a nightcap from the mini bar. I guess she's hoping it will help her sleep. I grab a beer for myself and settle back on my bed, flicking the channels on the TV until I find a cheesy movie. I'm pretty sure we'll both fall asleep before its ended.

Declan

I nod my head at the night security guard as I leave the hospital, heading out into the dark night. It doesn't take long to walk to the hotel which is conveniently located close by. Checking my watch, I see it's not quite as late as normal, that's good. I'm hoping that Holly will still be awake. I miss her, I know she's there for me, but I feel like I'm neglecting her in favor of Gran at the moment. It's not a choice I want to make. I want them both, but I think fate has taken that decision away from me.

Inserting my keycard in the door of the hotel room I ease it open slowly, just in case Holly is asleep already. I hear a low buzzing and can't quite place where it's coming from. I round the corner into the main part of the room and stop still, mesmerized by the sight in front of me.

Holly is laid back on the bed, her head thrown back in pleasure, her legs parted, knees high as she pleasures herself with a vibrator I'd taken on our holiday with us as a joke. What I'm watching is no laughing matter, it's hot as fuck. I must have made a noise as Holly suddenly jerks upright and looks as though she's about to scream the room down when she realizes it's me in front of her.

"What the fuck, Declan?" she screeches at me, tossing the vibrator guiltily aside.

"I'm sorry, baby," I laugh, "but that was hot as hell. Although I'm a little sad that you've replaced me already," I snicker.

"Pfft." Her retort makes me laugh harder. She moves across the bed until she's level with me and grabs a hold of my shirt, drawing me closer. "I'm glad you're here," she smirks. "The personal touch is so much better than self-service."

My little minx winks at me and I slowly unbutton my shirt. It's time to show my girl just how personal a service I can offer.

20

Cam

I'm not sure how well either of us slept last night, I know I tossed and turned for hours before it felt like I nodded off. The hotel bed was comfortable enough, I just think that there was so much going through my head. It felt like an internet browser with multiple tabs open, flicking from one concern to the next on repeat.

Sahara looks pretty refreshed, although she definitely has bed hair. She looks sexy as fuck even before she hits the shower. As she passes by the end of the bed I'm sitting on I have to stop myself from reaching out and touching her. I curse myself for not being a relationship type of guy. As hot as the sex was between us I can't go there again, firstly because I'm supposed to be protecting her, and secondly because she deserves someone who will treat her right.

The sound of the shower releases me from the spell I found myself in. I'm going to have to get a cold shower to ease off the hard on I've found myself with. It's not morning wood, my cock stood to attention as soon as it caught sight of Sahara as it always does these days. It sure is hard being around her.

I rush into the shower as soon as it is free, the last thing I need is to see her wrapped in a too small hotel towel. The spray of the shower feels great as it eases some of the tension from my neck, the water beating down quickly and force-fully. It's just what I need. My erection isn't going to go away anytime soon, so I jerk off under the cleansing stream. The relief is good, but my brain keeps telling me that fucking Sahara over the kitchen table was so much better. It's right, but it needs to shut up, I can't think like that. I've got a job to do.

The coffee shop attached to the hotel offers us a reasonable selection for breakfast, at least the coffee is strong. I almost inhale the first cup much to Sahara's amusement. Whilst I've ordered a full cooked breakfast to fuel me for the day she is toying with a bowl of yoghurt and granola. How can chicks eat rabbit food like that? I've never understood the appeal.

The seats around us are almost empty, most people having already left to get on with their day. I'd allowed us a bit of a lie in as I reckon we needed what little sleep we could catch up on, and the roads back to the farm will be a little quieter now the morning rush hour has passed.

My mobile dings with an incoming text and I smile when I see it's from Holly. She's checking in to see if Sahara feels up to a little shopping before we head back. I look over, but she's lost in her own world again, staring out of the window at the people passing by on the streets, although from the lack of emotion on her face I'm not sure how much of what she's seeing is being taken in.

"Sahara," I gently tap her arm to get her attention. As expected it provokes her to jump a little in her seat, the contact startling her. Deciding it's probably better to just show her the message I pass the phone over.

"I don't know," she sighs. "I'm not sure I'm really that bothered today."

I remind her of the lack of sleepwear and I'm guessing underwear, finally she capitulates. She agrees to an hour tops. I message Holly back and arrange to meet in the hotel lobby, allowing just enough time for me to finish my breakfast. A man's got to eat after all.

Sahara greets Holly warmly with a hug when she sees her and seems more animated around her than she does me. I guess I only have myself to blame for that.

I'm heading over to the hospital to see Declan before we leave when my phone rings. I'm half expecting it to be Holly to tell me that Sahara has changed her mind. I'm a little surprised to see that it's Greg, Jack Snrs right hand man.

"Hey Cam, how's it going?" His greeting is warm enough, but I can hear something in his voice that tells me that this isn't just a social call.

"Doing okay thanks," I offer, "Declan's still with his Gran and we're just hiding out at the farm mostly."

Greg clears his throat then comes out with the real purpose of the call. "I've been asking around and turns out Jerry has a bounty out on the both of you. Hundred grand for the girl to be returned to him and fifty grand for you to be wiped out." I'm almost offended at how cheap my life is; am I really worth so little. "I don't think Jerry realizes what you are," Greg laughs, "that's a pathetically low figure for your head." Greg has read my mind.

"What does it mean?"

"It means with that kind of money all he'll attract are idiots and time wasters. They'll be amateurs, but that makes them dangerous in their own right, they'll just focus on the payday and not on what damage they cause to anyone around you."

I'd figured as much, but it means we're now walking around with targets above our heads.

"Does he know we're staying in Harvey?" I'm desperately hoping the answer to that is no.

"I've heard a whisper that he does. That's the other reason that I'm ringing you," Greg replies. Shit! That is not what I wanted to hear. "Then again, there are rumors you're in Perth, Melbourne, Severed and a handful of other places. Just be on the alert. Do you need anything?"

We chat a little about what he thinks Jerry might be planning, but everything so far is still rumor and speculation. He hasn't been able to locate the house or warehouse where the girls are being kept, which is disappointing. If we have to go to war with Jerry I fully intend to hit him where it will hurt most, his trafficking business. No one so far has been prepared to come forward and admit to Jack Snr that Jerry is dealing in trafficking, but Greg is confident that someone will if he applies the right pressure. We just need solid evidence to ensure that Jack won't have cause to retaliate if we take Jerry out.

I've barely had chance to hang up the phone with Greg when it rings again, this time it's Chris to advise the truck with the hardware will be arriving at the farm this afternoon. That's good news, at least we can hole up and bunker in once that has arrived. Hopefully Holly and Sahara won't take too much longer, and we can head back and meet up with Chris's guys.

I have just enough time to call in and see Declan to catch him up on this morning's conversations when the girls return with armfuls of shopping bags. As expected most of them belong to Holly, but I'm pleased to see that Sahara has a decent amount this time.

Ever the gentleman I take them from her and go load up the truck. When I've finished Sahara is already in the passenger seat with her seatbelt fastened. I've just started the engine when she reaches for the flyer that I threw on to the dashboard last night. I'm about to tell her it's nothing when she lets out a muted scream and goes sheet white.

Snatching the now scrunched up paper from her tightly grasped hand I unfurl it slowly. Shit. It's a photo of Sahara at the hospital yesterday and right over her head there's a crudely drawn bullseye.

"Why did I think I could escape?" she sobs into her hands.

"Don't worry, I'll protect you," I try and reassure her. She looks up at me, defeat written all over her face.

"You have no idea what you're dealing with," she retorts.

She's right, I don't. But then again, Jerry and his cohorts

have no idea who they're dealing with. Shit's about to hit the fan and it's damn sure going to be us throwing it.

I spin the wheels of the truck as I tear out of the car park, eager to get back to the farm and start planning. It's time to call the guys in, and it's time to go find Jerry. I'm going to end this once and for all.

21

Cam

The journey back to the farm was as quiet as the one to the hospital. It's as though a steel resolve fell over Sahara once she snapped at me that I didn't have a clue what Jerry was like. This wasn't the time to tell her about my background, and why Jerry is most definitely going to end up on the losing side of this scenario. We never filled the girls in on what happened when I went to see Jack Snr, and I don't see any reason to change that now.

As I drive I mentally calculate my options. I'll call the guys when we get back and Sahara is out of earshot, we need to take the battle to Jerry and not just risk him finding us at the farm. I'll have to let Fred know what is happening, so he can alert the rest of the farm hands and make sure they're armed and aware. Hopefully between what they already have and the truck full of goodies arriving this afternoon we'll have more than enough supplies; worse case Chris is a veritable one-man armory and he'll soon get us what we need.

The more I think about the trafficking element of Jerry's business the more I want to get my hands on the guy. How many more girls like Sahara has he taken and destroyed. How many came from good, loving families? How many were destitute and picked up from the streets?

My sixth sense kicks in and I now know we're being watched. I knew I should have trusted my gut on the earlier journey, just because you can't see something doesn't mean it doesn't exist. If we're being watched then hopefully it means we're being followed. If they follow us back to the farm I can find them and get some intel. The advantage of having been a part of a special forces unit is that we don't just know how to fire weapons, we're trained in all sorts of fields. Luckily for me, and unluckily for whoever is following me, interrogation is one of my specialties.

Eventually the silence stops being my friend and I reach for the radio, country music filling the cab of the truck. Sahara is staring out of the window still, but I can see the almost imperceptible tapping of her foot in time with the track playing. For now, I'll take that. I hope that one day soon I'll be able to make her feel safe and put the smile back on her face.

Pulling up outside the farmhouse I see that Chris's guys are already here. I recognize them as the ones that dropped the gear off originally. Sahara makes her excuses and heads into the farmhouse whilst I show the guys over to the empty shed I'd already decided would be a perfect storehouse. They help me unload and offer to take the hire vehicle back now we have the truck from Chris as well. It will save me a journey, and hopefully means that whoever has been tracking us will take a while to catch up with us again.

As I watch the dust follow the departing truck I get out my phone to call Luke, Ryan and Jacko, the guys that made up the rest of our unit in Afghanistan alongside Max and Declan. We're a close-knit group, and whilst everyone has almost settled back into civilian life we'd all promised to be there for each other if needed. Declan was the first one to have to call in the favor back in Severed when a group of wannabe drug dealers threatened the safety of his new home town, now just weeks later I'm having to call them back to help me fix my mess. As good as it will be to see them again, I feel guilty at needing to call them here for this.

As I expected my request is met with nothing but agreement, we're a lot closer to them here in Harvey than we were in Severed so they'll all be here by the morning. I miss the way we used to work so closely together, almost reading each other's minds out on a mission. We're a well meshed team, and unfortunately for Jerry we're a deadly combination when we get together.

I'm not sure how much to tell Sahara of what's happening, but I think I need to let her in. She's seen the note and she already has first-hand knowledge of what Jerry is capable of. What she doesn't realize is that Jerry is outgunned, outmanned and out skilled. It's just a matter of time before we catch up with him.

I hope she'll be able to tell me something about his operation, whilst I appreciate that this is going to be difficult for her to talk about, we need the intel to help us move forward and stop Jerry. That could be an interesting conversation, and perhaps I should wait till the guys are here in the morning before attempting it. She's obviously still uncomfortable around me, and I can't blame her. I also can't give her false hope. I'm not a settling down type of guy.

I hear a clatter from the front of the shed where I'm rearranging supplies. At this time of day no one should be out here on the farm, and I'm pretty sure that Sahara won't venture out here. I pause, listening for any sign that something is out of place. There's another noise, so subtle I almost don't hear it. Someone is in here with me.

I ease stealthily around the crate I've been inspecting and on silent feet move closer to the door, all the time remaining hidden in the shadows. The guy in front of me is good, he's practically impossible to see, but he doesn't know that this is what I've been trained for. I sneak behind him and have my switchblade knife at his throat before he's even realized I'm there.

I've not seen the guy before, but with Jerry's bounty he could be just a goon for hire, one of Jerry's guys, or possibly just be one of the farmhands as well I guess, I haven't met them all yet, but the way he was sneaking around tells me otherwise.

One hand maintaining the knife at his throat, I use the other to pat him down. He's armed. It's a nice little .22, easy to hide, light to carry and a dream to shoot. I don't miss the knife in the holster at his ankle, slipping that into the back of my jeans. Once I'm happy that I've disarmed him I move him over to an old kitchen chair that had been abandoned in here. As we pass one of the boxes I grab a handful of cable ties, using them to secure him to the chair, none too gently. His wrists and ankles are tight to the chair arms and legs, with no room to wriggle out of them they're actually digging into his skin.

He sneers at me when I move to stand in front of him. "Do you know who you're dealing with?" He cocks his head to one side, appraising me. The look of disgust on his face won't be there for long once I've started on him.

"An amateur," I offer, "not a particularly good one at that." He isn't happy with my answer and tries to physically lift the chair and himself to lunge at me. Not happening. Before he can get any momentum, I've pushed him back down again.

I lean down and stare right into his eyes, they're cold and without fear which tells me this probably isn't one of Jerry's goons but someone on the trail of the bounty. He spits in my face and I leave the spittle there, not showing any reaction to his stunt.

"Now let me tell you how this is going to go," I reach behind me and pick up the cordless Black and Decker drill I had been using to open some of the crates, relishing the weight of it in my hand, replacing the .22 I'd taken from my prisoner. His face registers confusion at the change in weapon. I can see him relax a little into the chair as soon as I put the gun down. Now that was a mistake on his part. The game I'm planning on playing is going to hurt a lot more than one little .22 bullet. "I don't know if you ever read about the IRA back in Northern Ireland during the troubles?..." I pause, giving him a moment to reflect on his answer. He shakes his head. I didn't think he would have done, like me he's too young to have grown up hearing about them on the news, but unlike me, he's never read up on militia history. "Let me enlighten you," I offer, my teaching voice coming through strong, "if someone committed a crime back then they took the law into their own hands. You ever heard of kneecapping?"

"Of course I have," he looks at me disdain plain as day on his face. "I'm a professional, you're not going to scare me with your stories." He's confident and full of false bravado, I'll give him that, both of which will cause him more pain. I can't stand arrogance, especially when it's as misplaced as it is right now.

"Well," I continue, "whilst the most common practice was to shoot the knee out from behind, my favorite option is the drill. You can repair a knee shot out from behind, but you go at it with a drill..." I pause for dramatic effect waving the power tool in front of me. "Well, let's just say that's not going to be fixable and will hurt a fuck of a lot more."

His face shows no emotion. He's not scared that's for sure, he should be though. This is going to hurt, a lot! The fact he shows no emotion tells me he is some kind of professional, but the way he fumbled around in the shed when he came in also tells me he's not that good. I suspect most of the time he just takes his target out with his shiny little guns from a safe distance.

I hold the release button in on the drill then press the power switch, the drill vibrates to life in my hand, the whirr of the drill vibrating through my hand. I move steadily closer to him. He doesn't flinch.

"So, tell me where Jerry has the rest of the girls hidden," I ask calmly.

"Fuck off," he spits his response at me, spittle hitting the floor at my feet.

Moving closer I touch the drill bit against the arm of the chair, close to where his hand is bound, applying just enough pressure for the bit to bite into the wood and create a perfect hole. Still he doesn't flinch. That's okay, I have the rest of the day if needed.

It takes an hour of questioning and teasing with the drill before I establish he really is just a hired gun with no knowledge of Jerry's activities. It then takes just seconds to shatter the kneecap of his left leg. I've taken the precaution of stuffing a rag in his mouth to stifle the scream that I knew would come. It's incredibly painful and crippling. The crunch of the bone as it shatters is slightly sickening. I'm surprised at how hard it was to drill the kneecap, and at how little blood there was compared to my expectation.

His head has bobbed forward, the pain knocking him out. I slap his face until he comes around a little, then repeat my question. "Where does Jerry keep the girls?"

I can barely hear his response and ask him to repeat it. He genuinely doesn't know. I stare at him coldly, considering my options. If I let him go I'll have to take him to a hospital, he'll live, but he'll never walk properly again. If I let him go he'll talk, and maybe even find a way to seek revenge.

I picture Sahara in my mind's eye, and all the other girls that Jerry has taken, abused and sold. The answer is clear. I move slowly to the crate behind me, swapping the bloody drill for the .22 I took from him. I turn and face him. He can barely lift his head, but I admire the courage he finds to look me right in the eye as I pull the trigger, the bullet hitting square between his eyes and ending the risk he poses to the woman I promised to protect at all costs.

22

Cam

J'm trying to clean up the mess I made when Fred walks into the shed. Shit, I thought I'd made sure no one was around. He looks dispassionately at the body still slumped in the chair, held up only by the tie clips I'd secured him with.

"I'm guessing you're going to need some help cleaning up?" No questions, no fear. Fred obviously has hidden depths.

"Yeah, if you don't mind," I gesture to the pen knife that's just out of my reach. "I guess you want to know what's going on?"

Fred shakes his head. "None of my business, you can tell me if you want, but you're Declan's friend, you're practically family here. I trust that you did what you needed to in order to keep everyone safe." Without batting an eye, he passes me the knife so I can cut the body loose, then moves to the back of the shed and rummages around a little, coming back with a wheelbarrow and a tarpaulin. "There are some spades in the other shed, I reckon between us we can have this sorted before it gets dark."

I'm a little in awe of how calmly Fred is taking everything in. There's more to him than I thought. We'll get to the bottom of that later I'm sure.

We work side by side for the next few hours and when we're finished there's no trace that the guy ever visited the farm. Fred had found his vehicle parked on the farm's main approach road and persuaded a couple of the farm hands to drive it a few towns over and dump it with the keys in the ignition.

When we're done we head back to Fred's house where we sit on the porch, beer in hand and I tell him about the mess we've found ourselves in. He takes it in without blinking an confirms that he's ex-military himself, he came to work on the farm when he was discharged and now it's his home. As far as he's concerned Declan is his kin, and whatever we need, he'll support us. He's appalled at what happened to Sahara and suggests that when we've finished our beers we go have a chat with her together and see if we can find out more information on Jerry's operation. I'm honest with him about sleeping with Sahara and once he's finished telling me what a prat I am, he suggests to me that I need to make it up to her. I've not behaved like a gentleman, as if I didn't know that, and I need to apologize without putting my foot in it again if possible.

Beers finished we head over to the farmhouse in search of

Sahara. The house is in silence, but we find her seated at the kitchen table, an untouched drink in front of her. She looks to be lost in that world of her own again.

"Miss?" Fred knocks on the door frame to get her attention. She comes around from whatever fugue she was in and looks at us both.

"Hi Fred," she smiles warmly at him. "Cam." Her greeting to me is cooler and accompanied by a small nod of her head to acknowledge my presence. "Want to tell me what's going on out there guys?"

I look at her, what did she see or hear that has her questioning us?

"I'm not stupid," she acknowledges my unasked question. "I heard enough guns around Jerry to recognize the sound of one. Have they found us?" Her voice is resigned.

Deciding that honesty is the best way forward in this situation Fred and I sit at the kitchen table and fill her in on what happened earlier.

"So, he knows where I am?" she sighs. "I haven't got the energy to run anymore."

"You don't need to run," Fred reassures her, "Cam here has a plan, and I can guarantee that everyone here on this farm will do everything we can to keep you safe." He reaches over and places his large calloused hand on hers. She doesn't flinch from his touch like she does mine.

"Thank you," she almost whispers her response.

It's Fred who broaches the subject of Jerry's location with

her. "I know this is going to be hard for you, Sahara, but we need to know everything you can tell us about Jerry and his operation, even the smallest detail that you think is insignificant might be important and help us stop him from hurting you or anyone else again."

Sahara tells us how Jerry manipulated her life to the point she found herself homeless and jobless. He'd been pursuing her for over a year, and she'd managed to stay strong and avoid him but reached a point where she couldn't carry on anymore. She refuses to discuss her past before this, just telling us it's too painful and not relevant.

Its not clear why Jerry didn't just kidnap Sahara as that seems to be his modus operandi with most girls, although some he lures in from the streets. Perhaps he gets a sick thrill from breaking them down and getting them to beg him for help.

Jerry's goons had appeared the morning she found herself thrown out of the last hotel she'd called home, they found her standing on the sidewalk with only a measly box of possessions. She'd been bundled into the back of a car with blacked out windows so wasn't sure of the route they'd taken to the safe house.

The girls were kept in a large warehouse with armed guards on duty twenty-four seven. There were no luxuries, just thin mattresses on cheap camp beds in a large communal room and a basic bathroom with a rusty shower. There was no privacy as even in the bathroom guards were watching.

"Some of the girls were drug users, I can understand why," she tells us. "Anything that would blot out what was happening to us and around us would have been welcome."

She shudders at the memory, I want to draw her in my arms and reassure her that she's safe here, but her posture shows that's the last thing she wants right now whilst she relives her nightmare. "The drug users were the ones with the fastest turnaround, they weren't worth much, so he'd pimp them out to the cheap sick bastards and not ask questions if they didn't make it back in one piece." She starts to cry as she tells us about one girl called Maisie who came back so beaten and bruised one day that she didn't survive the night. She'd died in Sahara's arms, her pleas for pain relief ignored. There were so many broken bones and cuts on her body it's a wonder she survived as many hours as she did.

As Sahara describes outrage after outrage I clench my fists, I need to hit something as anger floods my veins. I can see Fred is trying to hold his fury back as well. The last thing Sahara needs right now is an outburst from either of us.

"The more well to do girls were sold to order, the day of the sale they'd have a hairdresser and make-up artist come in and make them look presentable, then be dressed in expensive but revealing lingerie, similar to the outfit I was wearing the night you found me." She looks embarrassed as she recalls the outfit that showed off just what an amazing body she has. Those girls never came back, although there were whispers that not all of them survived," she shudders and wraps her arms around herself. I really want to reach out and comfort her, but I'm scared that she'll reject me and not continue her story.

"I don't know where the warehouse is, but I can tell you it's about a twenty minute drive from where you found me."

Fred and I ask question after question of her for the next hour or so, trying to get every snippet that we can that will help in our search for the warehouse. The more intel I can get from her the more chance Chris will have of using his technology to pinpoint the location. By the time we're finished she's exhausted, her head is drooping, and her eyes are heavy.

Fred bids us goodnight and after making sure the doors and windows are all secured I escort Sahara up to her room.

"Can you stay with me tonight?" Her voice is so quiet and yet so desperate. "Reliving the warehouse and everything, I'm sure I'll have nightmares. I'm scared he's going to find me and take me back." Her whole body shivers. I can't imagine how scared she is to be asking me to stay with her as she hates the sight of me right now, but there's no way in hell I'm going to refuse her tonight.

Sahara heads into the bathroom and I take the opportunity to ring Chris and tell him what we know, he promises to get onto it straight away for us and let us know what he finds as soon as possible. It's time we take this battle to Jerry. We could just take Jerry out, but I have a burning need to end the trafficking first, besides hard evidence will make it easier for Jack Snr to support our actions.

Sahara comes out of the bathroom, her hair damp from the shower and dressed in full length pajamas. She still looks sexy as fuck to me. She stares hesitantly at the double bed then back at me. "It's okay, I'll behave myself." I promise her.

Pulling back the covers she lays down on the mattress, curling her body up into a defensive position. Removing my jeans and shoes but leaving my t-shirt and boxers on I crawl in beside her, pulling her close and finally allowing myself to comfort her. I can hear her cry herself to sleep, and all I can do is whisper soft promises that I will keep her safe and protect her with my life.

One thing is for sure, I'll personally see to it that Jerry never bothers her again.

23

Cam

I stir as I feel the warmth from the light reflecting through the window. At the side of me Sahara is still deep asleep, nestled into me. I hold my breath not wanting to disturb this moment. I'm not a relationship guy and don't do sleepovers so this is the first time I've woken up at the side of a woman, and I'm surprised at how natural it feels.

Sahara looks so peaceful, more peaceful than I've seen her since we met. A warm feeling goes through me that I'm the reason she looks that way, she obviously feels safe in my arms. Inwardly I curse myself for unintentionally hurting her, it's the last thing I'd want to do to this beautiful fragile creature who is slowly breaking down all my barriers. I wish I could be more for her, but I can't see how I can change the habit of a lifetime.

Slowly I raise my arm and check the time on my watch. It's

just before five am which means the farm hands are going to be arriving any time now. I can hear the faint clatter of pots and pans in the kitchen. I'm pretty sure that the noise will wake my sleeping beauty, I wish I could find a way to let her sleep. It's the only time I've seen her relaxed.

She still wouldn't tell us about her past last night, and I understand that. I need to earn back her trust, I just hope that in the meantime she'll open up to Holly. I want to fix her, but I can't until I know what's broken. She's holding so much pain inside it reminds me of Declan. I'm scared of what will happen if she doesn't let it out.

The clatter of boots in the kitchen below rouses her and she looks around her drowsily. Instead of the look of horror I expected to see on her face she looks at me warmly, even giving me a gentle smile. I need to be careful, this girl is slowly capturing my heart and I can't let that happen. She deserves better than me.

"I'm hungry," as she says that her stomach rumbles loudly, reaffirming her statement. I chuckle, and she swats at me in mock disgust. When I let out a matching but louder rumble she laughs out loud.

"I think we should go down and get some breakfast," I suggest.

"You figure?" She can't stop laughing at me, and the sound fills my soul with joy. I want to find a way of making her laugh like that all the time.

Luckily by the time we've showered and dressed there's still plenty of food left for us and for the first time I recall Sahara tucks into a hearty breakfast, leaving an empty plate.

It's mid-morning when we hear the sound of a vehicle approaching outside. Sahara looks concerned, but when I look out the window as it pulls up I let out a whoop. It's the guys. Grabbing hold of her hand I drag her with me outside to greet them.

Jacko, Luke and Ryan are stretching out after being cooped up in the car. It's a small hatchback and I look at it in surprise.

"Don't diss my car you jerk!" Jacko hisses at me.

"That's not a car it's a bloody matchbox," I can't help laughing.

"It's fucking uncomfortable is what it is," Ryan tells us, cricking his neck dramatically.

"Look, I don't need anything bigger in the city and it got us here just fine," Jacko retorts.

There's some good-natured ribbing between us all then Sahara steps forward.

"Sahara let me introduce you to this bunch of reprobates," there's a few mutterings from the guys about my opinion of them but they all step up and hug her warmly.

"Jacko here, the owner of this lovely tin can on wheels and the scruffiest guy amongst us is training to be a vet." Jacko bows dramatically from the waist.

"Luke is the quiet one of us, but probably the deadliest." Luke nods his head in greeting.

"And as for Ryan here, you need to watch out for him. He thinks he's a lady's man." Ryan flashes that cheeky grin of his at Sahara and she giggles in reply. We can't see his eyes behind the dark sunglasses that he always wears but I'm sure they're appraising her and calculating how quickly he can get her into his bed. "And Ryan, I add, "Sahara is out of bounds."

"Aww spoilsport," he retorts whilst reaching for Sahara's hand and placing an exaggerated kiss on it.

Fred has obviously seen the arrival of our guests and is heading over the yard to meet us. Sahara spots him and suggests that she'll go make drinks for us whilst we catch up on the events of yesterday.

It doesn't take long to bring the guys up to speed on what's been happening. They report that they didn't see anything suspicious on the way to the farm, and that the perimeter looks secure. We're all in agreement that the best course of action is to go on the offensive rather than watching our backs all the time.

We head out to the shed and check out the toys from Chris whilst we wait for him to ring us with an update.

❦

It's late afternoon when Chris finally rings with his findings. There's good news and bad news, he thinks he's located the warehouse, but Jerry appears to be off the radar. Fred's wife has taken Sahara to see the new foal that graced us with its presence this morning, so we're able to strategize in peace.

As much as I want to accompany the guys, we all agree that Declan and I should stay here, he needs to be with his Gran right now and I have to look after Sahara. Jacko, Ryan and Luke will go do recon and report back.

I call Greg to let him know what we've found out and he offers the use of Jack Snr's jet again which we gratefully accept, the sooner we get there the sooner we can find out what's happening and put an end to it. The jet will be here in the morning, allowing us the evening to catch up with each other.

Sahara seems much more relaxed around the guys than I expected her to be, she's animated and joins in the conversation, although she refuses any alcohol. She's also ignoring me. Its subtle and the guys haven't noticed, but I have. I guess that despite last night I'm still not forgiven. Guilt gnaws at me, and regret. I hate that I've brought this on myself. Maybe if we can resolve this situation with Jerry I'll be able to make my peace with her.

Despite the early start they're going to have in the morning its almost midnight before the evening ends. The guys have entertained Sahara with as many stories as they could remember that made me out to look like a dick. She laughs at them all. Utter bastards, if I didn't love them all so much I'd have to kill them and tell them so. That generates more laughter. She has an amazing laugh, her whole face lights up and her eyes sparkle. I feel like a caveman around her, my need to protect her is so strong. My cock on the other hand has other ideas. It desperately wants a repeat of the other morning. That can't happen again. It mustn't.

My resolve is tested to the limit as we reach the door to Sahara's room when I escort her up to bed and she asks me to stay with her again. I agree without thinking, the need to keep her safe overriding any common sense. As she snuggles back into me I can't stop my arms from wrapping themselves around her. She doesn't stop me, I lay awake, restless and tormented until I feel her finally fall asleep against me. Only then do I allow myself to doze off, my dreams haunted by images of Sahara.

24

Sahara

Cam is driving the guys to the airport this morning so asked me if I'd go spend some time with Holly to keep her company. Yeah, right, like that girl needs company. I know what he's angling for, he wants my story. I guess they deserve to know how I got myself into this mess with Jerry, and it will certainly be easier to tell Holly than Cam. Whilst I know deep down that I did nothing wrong, there's still guilt there, my parents drilled it into me. I guess the only thing to do is tell my story and see what happens next. Will any of them look at me in the same way when it's all come out?

This whole situation with Cam is breaking my heart even more, the way he rejected me cut deeply, and yet I can't stop my body yearning for his. This last couple of nights where he has held me as I've slept have been the best night's sleep

I've had in as long as I can remember. I feel safe in his arms. My body fits with his so well, and yet he insists that he's no good for me. I can't help feeling the reverse, that it's a case of I'm not good enough for him.

I'm glad to see that Holly has found a quiet corner in the coffee shop with comfortable sofas and low lighting. If I'm going to bare my soul, then this looks like a suitable location. Cam had rung her to say he was dropping me off, so she's already got the coffees in and I spy some blueberry muffins as well. Perfect.

Holly jumps up and hugs me enthusiastically when she sees me. I guess I never thought how lonely she must be at the moment with Declan spending all his time at the hospital with his Gran. I hug her back hesitantly, it feels like forever since I last had someone show me affection, it's almost as though I've forgotten how to respond.

Holly chatters away about the guys for a few minutes, until she looks at me and then pauses, head cocked to one side. "What's wrong? You look like you're going to be ill," she touches a cool hand to my forehead. "Are you okay?"

I guess the nerves about coming clean are showing. "I think I need to tell you my story..." I pause, waiting to see what her reaction is. I'm reassured when she doesn't sit and clap her hands in glee, instead expressing concern about my state of mind.

"Only if you want to," she puts her hand on top of mine, patting it slowly to reassure me. "It would help Cam and Declan if they knew what happened, but only when you're ready."

Once Holly has given me the opening I can't help the words that spill from my mouth. I tell her about Tom, getting pregnant and the whole scene at the hospital with his mother. Holly looks shocked, I wonder how she'll react when she hears what happened next?

"Telling my parents I was pregnant was one of the hardest things I've had to do. I really didn't expect the reaction I got. My Dad went ballistic, he picked me up by the arm and actually escorted me out of the house. He called me a jezebel and a harlot." Holly looks shocked that a parent could treat a child that way, I guess she's been luckier with family than I have. "You've got to understand," I try and excuse my Dad's behavior, "my parents are deeply religious and that's how they brought me up. I'd betrayed their beliefs and done the worst thing I could have done in their eyes. I'm not sure if it would have been any better if Tom was able to marry me, but for me to be a single mother was a sign that I belonged to the Devil." Not only had my Dad escorted me out of the house he'd made sure I understood that I was now dead to them, they wanted nothing to do with me or my bastard and I was never to darken their door again. They also told me they were cancelling the funding for my college degree.

"I tried to stay on at college, I really wanted to get my degree so I could support us both, and the college did everything they could, but without any money behind me I eventually realized I'd have to quit." That was a tough day for me, it felt a little like I'd given up on a dream. For as long as I could remember I'd wanted to be an accountant and run my own practice, now it was never going to happen.

"I found an apartment that I could just about afford by working in a local bar on an evening and a supermarket during the day. I was exhausted, but I squirrelled every penny I could away for when I had my baby so I could take care of her. I think the bar is where Jerry first found me, he kept hitting on me, but I ignored him."

Holly interrupts to ask what Jerry looks like, how do you describe just how repulsive someone is? "It's not just his appearance," I reply, "he's fat and sweaty and the thought of him touching me makes me shudder, but it's a vibe he gives off. I can't describe it, but it makes my skin crawl just thinking about it. Somehow, even back then before it all started I knew this man was someone I should avoid."

I think back to the little apartment I'd found and how happy I managed to be. It was only a little studio with a small bath-room, but it was everything I needed. Without medical insurance I couldn't afford doctors' appointments so visited the library every chance I could to read up on what I needed to do for my baby.

"When I went into labor the old lady who was my land-lady and lived next door to me came and helped, I couldn't afford the hospital, Nellie sat with me for hours and held me when the contractions wracked my body, but it was worth it when I laid eyes on my daughter for the first time."

"But,..." Holly interrupts. "I thought you lost your baby?"

Relief floods her face when I reply. "No, she was a healthy 7lb baby. I loved her so much, I couldn't believe it was possible to love someone that much but as soon as those baby eyes looked at mine I was a goner. I swore I'd do anything and everything to protect her." My voice breaks as I talk about her. The memories are bittersweet.

Holly's face is a mass of unasked questions. I know she's burning to ask what happened next, but our coffee cups are empty, and she offers to go refill them. Its good timing, whilst she's gone I manage to draw in a deep breath and calm the inner turmoil that threatens to come to the surface and leave me a blubbering mess.

I take a sip of the burning coffee and continue my story.

"Thanks to Nellie I managed to carry on working at the supermarket, she'd look after Sophia for me during the day and refused to take any money for it. All she asked in return was sharing a meal or two with her, so she had some adult company. She was doing me a favor really as those meals with her were the only time I could afford to eat properly. The rest of the time I ate snacks or the cheapest food I could find. Any spare money went on Sophia."

"Sophia would have been about two when Nellie died, luckily it was during the night when Sophia was with me, she passed in her sleep. I hadn't realized how close I'd grown to Nellie, she was the grandma I never had, and adored Sophia. It was mutual. I like to think that Sophia made her last few years happy ones." I pause again, wiping a tear from my face at the memories of Nellie.

"I hadn't known that Nellie had a grown-up son, apparently they were estranged since he got married. His wife hadn't cared for Nellie and did everything she could to keep her out of their lives. They'd had children that Nellie never got to meet, which was such a shame as she was so good with Sophia. Anyway, he turned up one day and told me I'd have to leave. He was selling the house and didn't want lodgers getting in the way of the sale. That's when my life started to spiral out of control."

I go quiet as I remember the worst time of my life. I struggled to find somewhere to live that I could afford, and when I did, they refused to allow Sophia to live with me. It was a strict no pets or children policy. I couldn't afford childcare, so I could get a better job, and was stuck. I did the only thing I could think of, I called my parents and asked for help.

"I was so naive, " I continue my story, "when they pulled up outside I actually thought my life was going to get better, instead their solution broke my heart. My Dad told me that I was still dead to them, but that they wouldn't see Sophia suffer because of my sin. Can you believe that? My own father turned his back on me. My parents offered to take Sophia to live with them on the farm, they'd raise her as their own and give her a good life, but there was a condition." I stop, tears now flowing more freely down my face. "I was never allowed to see her again, she was never to know that I was her mother." Holly starts crying now, and pulls me into her arms, holding me close and gently patting my back to comfort me. It takes a while for me to pull myself together before I can continue my story.

"I had no choice, I had to do what was best for Sophia even if it broke my heart. Waving goodbye to her was the worst thing I've ever had to endure, knowing I'd never see her again. I grieve for her every day. She's too young to remember me, and that hurts. But I know she'll have a good life." No matter how many times I tell myself the sacrifice I made was the right choice it still hurts.

"I took the cheap apartment and managed to get my job back at the bar. I figured if I kept myself busy I wouldn't be able to think about how much I missed Sophia, and I saved every penny I could, so I could go back to college. I hoped that if I managed to get my life back on track then somehow, I might be able to persuade my parents to let me have her back. Then Jerry happened..."

I take a sip of coffee steeling myself for what comes next. "Over the next few months he appeared more and more, he made no secret that he wanted me, but I managed to hold him off. That's when he got wise and overnight I lost both my jobs and my home. I'm not sure how he did it, probably threatened the managers, it's his style after all. I ended up on the streets. I managed to find cheap hotels for a while but it's scary how quickly my savings disappeared. When I found myself sat on a bench in the park with no money, no home and no Sophia I finally gave in. This was no life anymore and I naively thought that Jerry couldn't be worse than what I was currently facing."

"The day I walked into the pub and told Jerry he'd won was the end for me. I had no fight left in me. I know Cam thought I was on drugs the night he rescued me, he was wrong. I'd just become so numb, I refused to allow myself to feel anymore. I didn't even cry when the girls I was held captive with didn't come back. I was just resigned that this was going to be my fate as well, and in some perverse way just hoped it would happen sooner rather than later."

Holly looks at me in horror, there are tears on both our faces. She hugs me so tight I'm scared she's going to break me.

"It's going to be alright, Sahara," she coos. I'm not sure who she's trying to convince, me or her. "Our wounded heroes will fix all this, I know they will." She hugs me tighter and that's how Cam finds us when he walks into the coffee shop.

I look up at him and wonder if he really is my hero, or is he just going to break my heart even more than it already is.

25

Sahara

The drive back to the farm seems like as good a time as any to tell Cam my story. Now I've told Holly I don't think it will be as hard. I'm wrong. Cam's face goes through various stages of anger as I relate my tale. At times his hands grip the steering wheel so tightly they go white. He also mutters more than one 'bastards' at various stages as I talk.

The one thing he doesn't make me feel is guilt. We're pulling into the farm by the time I finish telling him about becoming Jerry's possession and how it came about. When we pull up he's out of the truck so fast I think I must have upset him. Seconds later he's at my side of the vehicle and has opened the door. He pulls me out and holds me in a tight embrace.

"We'll fix this Sahara, I promise you," he whispers into my hair. "We'll fix this."

As strong as I managed to be whilst I told Holly and then Cam about Sophia, I can't maintain it anymore. I almost collapse as the grief takes hold and I start sobbing heavily. Cam doesn't hesitate, he lifts me into his arms and carries me up to my room. The whole time I cry into his shoulder, tears wracking my body.

He places me on the bed then crawls on next to me, drawing me into his arms, uttering soothing words I can't hear above my crying. He just holds me close. It feels like I cry forever, but eventually there are no more tears. When I've finally stopped crying I feel movement as Cam leaves the bed. He's abandoned me, and if I had anymore tears left I'd be crying still. How could he?

Before I know it, Cam has returned, a damp washcloth in his hand. He sits beside me and gently wipes the drying tears from my face with the cool cloth. Its soothing. It's also such a thoughtful thing to do. When he's happy that he's cleaned my face up he draws me back into his arms. I'm so exhausted from my crying that I fall asleep.

When I wake I think it must be late afternoon. Cam's still there beside me, his arm still holding me close. I've never known anyone like him, there's something so natural about being here in his arms. I feel safe. If I'm honest, here in his hold is the only place I do feel safe. I can't work out why he's here with me, why he wants to help me, why any of them do for that matter.

I've been abandoned by my own family so why would these

strangers feel they need to take care of me? It doesn't make sense. The only other person who showed me kindness was Nellie. I miss her so much. It's no good getting close to anyone, life has decided that for some reason I don't deserve that. Anyone I get close to dies or leaves me. Yet, knowing that, I can't help the way I feel about Cam.

I decide then and there that despite knowing he will leave me, I am going to fight for Cam. I'm not going to let him push me away. If life is going to treat me like shit again, then I at least deserve a little happiness before it comes to pass.

I take in Cam. He looks so peaceful as he sleeps, I could watch him all day. His chest rises and falls in a slow hypnotic rhythm. I take my hand and place it over his heart, the reassuring beat beneath calming me. He must sense my touch as his eyes slowly open.

"Hey, how did you sleep?" his voice so full of concern that I almost convince myself he really does care for me.

"Better with you here," I answer honestly.

Cam's about to say something but I silence him with my finger on his mouth. Suddenly feeling brave I lean in and replace my finger with my lips. He responds to my kiss, its slow and sensual. I can feel the heat of my arousal between my legs, it's almost like a physical ache. I need this man. Cam pulls away from the kiss and I feel regret that he's not into this moment, but its short lived. He looks at me with such passion it fills me with hope.

His hand traces my face, his touch so gentle, and he brushes some hair away from my face.

"We can't," he whispers. "I'm no good for you."

"We can," my voice is so firm I almost don't recognize it. "I need you Cam. I'll take whatever I can, I know it can't last, but right now, I need you."

Cam groans and I think he's going to pull away from me, instead he pushes me onto my back and kisses my face and my neck. I wrap my legs around his back, afraid that he'll change his mind, and desperate to keep him close. I can feel the press of his erection between my legs and the ache for him to be inside me is stronger than ever.

Cam takes his time to unbutton my blouse, placing kisses against my flesh every time he reveals more of me. My body feels like its burning up beneath him. I can feel the press of his weight against me, but he's not heavy. It feels just right. When he reaches my breasts, he pulls down the lace of my bra, exposing my nipple which he draws into his mouth. The sensation shoots all the way through me to my core. I can't tell who the groans are coming from but I'm pretty sure it's the both of us.

My greedy hands reach down and try and undo the belt on his jeans. Why does he always have to wear a belt? Realizing what I'm trying to do he lifts up enough for me to get access. Once I've released his cock from his jeans he pushes me away, taking his time to undress me. I'm lying there naked on the bed and he's still got his clothes on. There's something a little unfair about this situation and I tell him so. Smirking he moves from the bed and slowly undresses before me. A male stripper couldn't have done a better job, and the tension in the room heightens as he returns to the bed, his magnificent cock bobbing before him as he approaches. I lick my lips in anticipation.

He kneels on the bed and crawls up towards me, stopping to

part my legs and lowers his head to my core. I gasp as I feel the gentle stroke of his tongue against my clit. His insistent tongue laps away and his hands reach up to play with my nipples. The sensation is too much, the combination causing a tremor to run through my whole body, but he doesn't stop, licking and teasing at the same time. My body can't take any more and my orgasm explodes through me, my whole body shaking beneath his touch. He lifts his head from between my legs and grins cheekily up at me.

"You enjoyed that then?" His chuckle vibrates through his body, I can feel it where his skin touches mine.

"Nah, not really," I cockily reply. He knows I'm lying.

Cam moves on top of me, kissing me, I respond greedily. I need more, that small taste of what he can do to my body not enough. I reach for his length, but he pushes my hand away. Is he rejecting me? Surely not.

"Later, there's plenty of time for that later," he promises, "right now I just need to be inside you." His words instantly put my mind at ease. There's nothing I want more right now.

Cam pushes into me, slowly at first, each movement taking him deeper and deeper until I can feel his balls against me. This is nothing like the other day, this is slow and sensual sex. As good as the kitchen table was, this is definitely the best sex I've ever had. Not that I have a lot to judge it against.

He takes his time, the slow pace only serving to increase the fire that burns within me, each thrust taking me closer and closer to my orgasm. He waits until my climax clenches his cock then enjoys his own release. The pulse of his orgasm and the accompanying sounds of satisfaction are the perfect ending. He collapses at the side of me, we're both a hot and sweaty mess, and pulls me into his side.

"Maybe that wasn't such a bad idea after all," he grins.

He's right, it wasn't. What he doesn't realize is that I'm not going to let that be a one off. It felt so natural and so right that I'm determined to make the most of it whilst I can. He may be an ex-soldier, but I don't' think he has any idea of the battle ahead with me. I'm not going to let him go easily.

26

Cam

The guys are flying back in to the airport on Jack Snr's jet, sounds like the recon went well and we need to sit down and decide what we do next. I've left Sahara at the farm, she's with Fred's wife looking after the new foal. I've left enough time to meet up with Holly before I need to be at the airport. I need her advice.

I park in the hospital car park and message Holly that I've arrived. We agreed to meet down here. I'm not sure I can handle visiting Gran, although I know I should be there for Declan. I'm a shitty friend.

Holly appears through the hospital doors and smiles widely when she sees me. She's the best thing to happen to Declan, she grounds him, and best of all she's helping him fight the demons he brought back from Afghanistan. She's given him a reason to live. I'll be forever grateful to her for saving my friend.

We end up in the same corner of the coffee shop she was in the day before yesterday with Sahara. It must be her favorite spot. I buy the coffees, remembering the muffin, and head over to join her.

We spend an hour discussing the story that Sahara told us. We're both appalled at the way her family treated her. I finally understand her reticence about the bike. Its how Tom ended up in hospital. We're both curious about what happened to Tom and Holly offers to look into it for me. She speaks with venom about Tom's mother and I don't blame her.

"She would have been full of grief," I try to offer an explanation.

"She's a total bitch and was bang out of order," Holly doesn't mince her words. That's the thing with Holly, you always know where you stand with her.

"How's she holding up?" Holly mumbles around the piece of muffin that she's just put in her mouth.

"She's doing okay, about what you'd expect. I'm taking care of her." I smile when I think of just how I'm taking care of her.

"Cam, you didn't!" Holly snaps at me. Shit, what did I say that gave it away? "I can't believe you slept with her again." The disappointment in her voice hurts.

"Why is that so wrong?"

"Because you don't do relationships, you're going to break her heart and she's too fragile for that you dick." She's right. I don't do relationships. I know I shouldn't be sleeping with her, that I'm giving her false hope, but I really can't help myself.

I try and explain myself to Holly but just end up sounding like even more of a shit than I did at the beginning.

To be fair to her Holly does try to get to the bottom of why I don't do relationships. I honestly don't know. Holly decides it's because I was in the military and I'm such a good guy that I didn't want to leave someone behind if anything happened to me. She really does like to see the best in people, but I'm not sure she's right on this one. I think it's something deeper, more selfish, but even I can't come up with a good enough reason why I couldn't try to make it work with Sahara.

We finish our coffee as its time for me to leave for the airport. I promise Holly that I'll be careful with Sahara, but right now I can't give her up.

The plane is taxiing along the runway when I arrive. The guys are in good spirits if a little tired. They managed to locate the warehouse. They think that there are at least a dozen girls in there at the moment, with as many guards. They'd watched the site for almost twenty-four hours and there seems to be a regular timetable for the switchover of Jerry's guys, although there was still no sign of him.

"They're amateurs for the most," Luke reports, "although a couple of them look like they might have had some training." The guards themselves aren't a concern, but what we need to be careful of is what happens to the girls inside when we make our move. We don't want them being used as hostages or human shields. We discuss whether this is something we should deal with ourselves or pass over to the authorities. The concern is that they would want to get the guys higher up the chain and that would mean an unacceptable delay. We've got photographic evidence for Jack Snr although we'd all have been happier if we'd been able to include Jerry at the site.

I'll report in to Greg when we get back to the farm and see if he has any news as to where the asshole might be hiding out. There's no danger of Jerry doing his own leg work, he won't want to get his hands dirty, but it is like the weasel to lay low. Whilst saving the girls is high on my priority list, catching Jerry and making him pay for what he's done to Sahara is much more important to me.

Sahara is on the porch waiting for us when we return. She looks pensive. "Did you find them?"

"Let's go inside and get something to eat then we can tell you what we found," Jacko offers. "It would be useful if you could tell us more about the set up inside if we've found the right place."

Sahara accepts the suggestion, looking hesitantly at me as we enter the house. She's worried that now I've been away I'll have changed my mind about her, I can see it in her face. I lean in and kiss her on the cheek, pulling her into my side. It seems to reassure her, and she smiles up at me as we head into the kitchen to eat.

Dinner seemed to last forever as there were so many questions for Sahara about the interior layout. At first, she'd apologized for not being able to remember much about her time in the warehouse, but as the meal progressed she seemed to recall more and more that she thought she'd forgotten. I suspect it was more that her mind had tried to block it out to protect her, understandable really.

The warehouse is pretty remote and set amongst several abandoned buildings so traffic in and out of the site doesn't appear to attract attention. It's close enough to Jerry's center of operations that he can manage the set up, but distant enough not to be suspicious. Sahara is biting her lip pensively trying to recall if she ever saw Jerry at the warehouse.

"I don't think he ever visited," she finally says. "It always seemed to be Steve."

That's the first time she's been able to give us a name and she looks slightly surprised that she knew it. She describes him to us and Luke nods his head as he recognizes the description. Thinking back to the night I met Sahara I'm sure the guy was in the room with us. She agrees. He's the one who'd brought her to Jerry for the evening.

Greg still has no news on Jerry's whereabouts, although as far as he's heard the bounty is still out on Sahara and me. We need to find Jerry and end this, I'm not going to risk any harm coming to her. I pass on the intel regarding the warehouse and he agrees to go talk to Jack Snr and see how he wants us to handle the situation. He thinks, as do we, that the best course of action is for us to go in there rather than report it. We know it means that the guys Jerry is selling to will just buy from somewhere else, but at least it will hopefully keep them at bay and keep Sahara safe.

Everyone is exhausted by the time the meal has finished so we call it a night. As we reach Sahara's door she pulls me into the room with her. I can't say no, but I know that I need to talk to her, to tell her how I'm feeling and that there isn't a future for us. But tonight, I can't bring myself to say the words, instead choosing to lose myself in her embrace. I know that makes me a total shit, and that Holly will have my guts for this, but I just can't help it.

27

Sahara

I could get used to waking up next to Cam, he's an addiction I don't want to break. He's still asleep and I lay there just watching him, appreciating the toned abs and strong arms, memories of our love making last night bringing a grin to my face. Cam can be such a gentle lover, and yet he can be rough as well, like that morning over the kitchen table. That was hot as hell.

I know he's going to leave me soon, he'll go with the guys to free the girls from the warehouse. I can't ask him not to go, but my heart is scared that he won't come back to me. Life has a habit of taking away anything that makes me happy, and Cam makes me happier than I've ever been in my life. He makes me feel wanted, and I can't recall ever feeling wanted before. My parents were good parents, but never made me feel that I was the best thing that had happened to them. I think I always felt a bit like an afterthought, they had each other and their God, and I came somewhere after that.

Cam stirs, but unlike the previous morning he doesn't reach for me. Instead he leaves the bed without a word and I can only presume he heads for the bathroom as he leaves the room. I lay in bed waiting for him to return, foolishly whiling away the time with images of a happy ever after with him. I know it can't happen, he's not that kind of guy, but a girl can dream.

He doesn't return.

I make my own way to the bathroom and find it empty. I scrub my skin angrily in the shower, taking out my temper on my delicate flesh. I knew this was coming but hadn't expected the rejection to be so soon. I'd hoped for a little bit longer at least. I'm so angry that I over do the shampoo then find my eyes stinging as the foam gets in my eye through my carelessness.

I hide out in the shower for as long as I can, the water starting to cool. He's not in my room when I return, and I chide myself for believing he would be. I comb the knots from my hair, deciding to let it dry naturally. I can't seem to find the enthusiasm to care about my appearance today, dressing in denim shorts and a crop t-shirt. I'll go and spend the morning with the foal, that should cheer me up.

Breakfast seems to be over when I make my way into the kitchen, so I just grab a coffee from the pot. I've lost my appetite anyway. The house sounds empty, so I decide to take my drink and enjoy it in the sun out on the porch swing.

Cam is already out there on his own, I thought he'd be off

somewhere with the guys. He tries to rise from the swing when he sees me, and I cut him off.

"Don't you dare walk away from me," cold anger lacing my voice. At least he has the decency to look ashamed.

"I'm sorry." His apology sounds genuine enough, but I don't want to hear it.

"Why?" I ask. "Why am I not good enough for you?" I'm fighting hard to keep the tears at bay.

"Not good enough?" he looks surprised at my words. "Sahara, if anything you're too good for me. You deserve someone who'll put you first."

"In my whole life no one has ever put me first," I snap at him. "Why should you be any different?"

"You deserve someone better."

"Who are you to decide what I deserve? I'm old enough to make my own decisions. I didn't think you were a quitter Cam, or afraid of a fight, yet you're being a fucking coward walking away from what we could be." I'm so angry I'm almost spitting the words at him.

"I'm not relationship material."

"You can't punish me for a mistake someone else made in your past, it's not fair on me. I'm not that person," I throw back at him.

"It's not like that, there wasn't anyone."

"Then what the fuck is it, Cam? We fit well together, we have amazing sex, what is it that stops you wanting to be with me? Is it my past?" I should have known my past was never going to let me be, I just wish I knew what I'd done that was so wrong I wasn't allowed to be happy.

Cam rises from the seat and moves towards me. Reaching out he wipes away the tears I hadn't realized were falling and I inwardly curse at this sign of my weakness. "It's not you, honestly, it's not you, it's not your past," he tries to explain. "I've never wanted a relationship, I've never looked ahead and wanted the whole white picket fence and kids like some of my friends do. I just don't know how to do relationships."

"And you won't even try?" I lift my head in defiance. "I thought you were a better man than that, Cam." With that I turn and walk away from him, ignoring him when he calls my name.

I practically run up the stairs and throw myself on the bed, letting the pent-up frustration manifest itself in a crying jag that I don't think is ever going to end.

Cam

I lower myself back onto the porch swing, head in hands and wonder if I've just made the biggest mistake of my life. I'm pretty sure I have. Off to the side I hear a cough, Fred is standing there watching me.

"How long have you been there?" I ask.

"Long enough to realize you're a bloody idiot," he shrugs his shoulders. "She's right, you're a better man than that."

"I've messed it up big time, haven't I?" Fred just nods his head in response.

Fred finally moves and comes to sit beside me on the swing. "Being in love isn't easy," he starts, "it's scarier than being on the battlefield. At least out there you know who your enemy is, you're trained how to respond to each situation. Love on the other hand, no one trains you for how to deal with that. I was scared silly when I met Edie."

"Really?" Fred doesn't strike me as the kind of guy to be scared of anything.

"Yep, put me in a war zone any day," he chuckles. "I was like you, too scared to commit, but luckily Edie decided she saw something in me worth fighting for and she eventually wore down my defenses." The grin on his face tells me he's recalling happy memories. "Don't get me wrong," he continues, "it's constant hard work. It's not all plain sailing, but if you treat a relationship like a partnership then you'll be fine. You'll have bad days and she'll be there for you, and you need to be there for her when she has bad days. You won't always get along, that's life and to be expected, just never go to bed angry with each other."

"I don't know if I can pull this one back." My fingers are playing with the bottom of my t-shirt, anything to avoid looking Fred in the eye and seeing his disappointment in me.

"Do you want to? Is she worth a fight?" Fred's voice breaks my fidgeting.

"Yeah, she's something special. She deserves better than me though."

"Piffle," I almost laugh at Fred's use of the word, it sounds like something his wife Edie would say instead. "You're a fine young man, I've known you for years, and I think you're just what that poor girl needs." He stands and starts to leave the porch. "Now man up and get yourself in there and make it right with her." With that he walks off towards the barn.

I sit and contemplate what Fred has been saying. I think he's right, I'm out of my depth and that's what scares me. I'm used to knowing exactly what to do in a situation. He's also right that I've been a bloody idiot. I just hope it's not too late to make it right.

28

Holly

*I*t's quiet when I enter the hospital room. I look over and see that Declan is asleep. He's pulled the chair next to the bed and his head is resting on the pillow next to his Gran, and his arm is across her. My heart almost breaks at the sight in front of me. It speaks of utter devotion.

I move across the room as quietly as I can, not wanting to spoil the moment. It's probably the best part of an hour that I sit and watch them, even the nursing staff haven't disturbed us. One of the nurses had popped her head around the door, but when she saw the scene in front of her she backed out and let the door close.

From the looks the nursing staff have been giving each other and the sympathy on their faces I'm guessing we're not going to have to wait much longer. I don't know how he's going to cope without her. He's been through so much already, and I'm scared that losing her is going to break him. I'll be there for him, but somehow, I don't think that's going to help.

It's still not been a year since I lost my brother and my best friend, and there are days where I don't want to get out of bed and face reality. I'm told that it gets easier with time, I'm not sure the pain gets any less, I think you just become used to carrying it around with you. Life has to go on, but there are days where I wonder why? Declan has helped me, but it doesn't cure the injustice that I still feel from losing them both. Why does life have to be so cruel. Look at what Sahara has been through, and her parents still believe that God is good? I don't believe in God, I can't. I believe in good and evil and that's as far as I can go. I can't bring myself to believe in something that would allow people to suffer so much.

Declan starts to stir, it takes him a while to notice that I'm in the room. He looks a little embarrassed when he sees me. My poor boy.

"Hey," he stands and stretches out his back then comes around the bed to kiss me. I throw my arms around him and hug him tightly. If I could take away the pain of what's to come for him I would.

A nurse pops her head around the door and seeing that Declan is awake now, enters the room. She carries out her checks, chatting away to Gran as though she was awake. When she's finished updating the charts she turns to me and offers me a drink. I'm not thirsty but thank her and accept, hoping that it will give me some distraction.

Declan follows her out of the room, I can hear the low

murmur of conversation outside the door, but not the words that are being said. When he returns he looks so lost that I immediately go to him.

"She said not to leave tonight," his voice breaks as he says the words. Every other night the nursing staff have told him it's okay for him to leave and get some rest, they'd call him if they need him. My strong man has tears in his eyes and the sight of them breaks my heart. "Stay with me?" he asks. "I don't think I can do this alone."

"Of course I will," I can barely get the words out, "should I call Cam for you?"

Declan looks confused. "I don't know, should I?"

"I'll call him, and he can make the decision, how's that sound?" Declan nods in agreement, returning to his chair at the side of the bed, and taking hold of his Gran's hand again. I let him know I'll be back soon and head outside to make the call.

"Cam," I can barely speak for the tears, "I think Declan's going to need you tonight," I sob.

"I'm on my way!" Cam doesn't need any explanation, it's enough for him to know that Declan needs him. I knew it would be.

I take a moment to try and compose myself before I return to the room, Declan doesn't need to see that I've been crying, although when I splash cold water on my face in the toilets it does little to disguise the fact.

Climbing those stairs back to her room is harder than I thought possible, and I never even met her. From everything I've heard I'd have loved her and her no nonsense approach to life. I already love her for having been there for Declan, for having had the strength to get him to see that life was worth fighting for when he returned from Afghanistan. I wish I'd had the chance to know her, to thank her.

The ward is quiet when I return, the changeover of staff is due soon. There's none of the jollity I've previously heard amongst the staff, it's like a shadow has fallen over them. I don't know how they can do their job, days like this must be particularly hard on them.

When I return to the room there's a coffee on the windowsill waiting for me. Declan hasn't moved from his chair, his head back on the pillow next to his Gran. I have to turn my back on them and look out of the window as the tears start again. I try and sip my coffee, but it doesn't taste right so I place it back on the windowsill.

There's a garden courtyard below and a young couple are sitting there, his hand on her heavily pregnant belly. The circle of life goes on, but right now I can't find any consolation in that.

The minutes drag, each hour ticking by so slowly I feel sure the clock has stopped. I sit there in silence, feeling a little like an intruder if truth be told. I'm not sure I belong here, but here I'll sit because Declan is going to need me soon. It's almost as though he's forgotten I'm in the room with him, his focus solely on his Gran. I wouldn't have it any other way.

The chair isn't the most comfortable, and as I fidget to get more comfortable I realize that I'm desperate for the bathroom. I quietly excuse myself. The walk back to the room goes too quickly, part of me hopes that when I return it's over, that I won't have to witness it, the other part of me knows how selfish that is.

When I return the scene is unchanged. I resume my seat by the window and wait.

The door opens and one of the nurses comes in. "I'm sorry to disturb you," she says in a soft voice. "I'm not on shift tomorrow, I just wanted to come say goodbye." Tears prick my eyes at her gesture. Declan finally rises from his chair and goes over to her. She gives him a hug and he thanks her for everything she has done for his Gran. I realize then that she's been on duty almost every day I've been here.

When the door closes behind her Declan resumes his seat. Taking his Gran's hand in his he talks to her.

"It's okay, Gran." his voice is husky and breaking, "you can let go now, go be with Grandpa. I love you, Gran." Declan rests his head on her chest and stays like that.

It's another hour before it happens. Her breathing becomes quieter, every so often she misses a breath and we look at each other, then she'll breathe again and we exhale in relief, until finally she misses a breath and there isn't another one. It's so peaceful, we look at each other in disbelief. When we're certain that there isn't going to be another breath I offer to go and get the nurse. As I'm about to exit the room I look back and see Declan kissing her goodbye. When I find the nurse on duty I can't get the words out, she can tell though by the tears pouring down my face. She follows me into the room and confirms what we already knew.

"She's gone," she straightens the sheets over Gran, as though she were still sleeping. "She's at peace now bless her, you can stay with her as long as you want." She leaves the room quietly.

I hear heavy steps as someone rushes down the corridor to the room, then Cam comes in. He's out of breath as though he's been running. He takes one look at the bed and knows. It's only when Cam pulls Declan into a hug that he shows any reaction.

My poor man breaks down into loud, heartbreaking sobs. I don't know what to do for him, so just move over to them. Cam opens his arms to draw me into them, and he holds Declan and I whilst we cry.

"I'm so sorry I was too late," his voice is breaking.

"You're here now," Declan tells him. "You're here now."

29

Holly

*D*eclan didn't want to stay at the hospital, he'd said his goodbyes and that was enough for him. "That's not Gran anymore," he explained. He carried the small bag of personal effects with him, they were just small things that Fred had brought in, such as toiletries. When the staff had asked if he wanted his Gran's wedding rings he'd declined. He wanted her to keep them, they'd meant so much to her in life he wanted her buried with them.

Cam had followed us to the cafeteria, and we sit there nursing cups of coffee that none of us want to drink. I think that even though we'd known this was coming we are all still in shock.

"I'll wait and tell Fred when I get back," Cam offers. It's too early in the morning to disturb anyone.

"How is everyone?" Declan asks, although I can tell his heart isn't in it. He's just going through the motions.

"They're well, you should see the tin can that Jacko drove up in," Cam laughs. His face falls as he seems to think this isn't the time for jollity.

"Don't," Declan tells him. "Don't behave differently to how you would normally, she wouldn't want that."

"Yeah, you're right," Cam responds. I envy him, he got to meet that amazing woman.

Cam falters, he's got something he wants to tell Declan, but looks torn as to whether he should. Declan makes it easier for him by asking what happened with the recon. The conversation is almost normal after that. Cam fills Declan in on the warehouse, and Declan agrees that it's down to the guys to go fix this rather than wait on the authorities.

"Give me a day to make arrangements, then I'm all yours," he offers. He looks at me as though waiting for a rebuke. I'm not going to disagree with him, I know my man and I know that this is probably the best way for him to deal with his grief and the anger at his loss, go take it out on some deserving bad guys. When I'd lost Justice and Danni I'd wanted to lash out and hurt someone.

Cam offers to stay over and go to the funeral director with him, but Declan tells him he doesn't need him to. I'll be with him. My heart warms at the acknowledgement that I'm there for him, I just wish it was under different circumstances.

I ask him how things are between him and Sahara. The look on his face says it all.

"What have you done now," I ask in despair.

" I fucked up again," before I can chastise him he rushes on, "but I'm going to make things right," he promises.

"Is she talking to you?" I ask, suspecting the answer will be no if he's fucked up again.

"Erm, no, not at the moment," he replies sheepishly. "Any tips?"

Before I can reply Declan surprises me by answering, "Break the door down and let her know you won't take no for an answer." I look at Declan in surprise.

"What?" he asks, "isn't that pretty much what you did with me?" He's right and I have to agree with his suggestion. Cam looks less convinced.

"Don't worry about the door, Gran would have given you the same advice." There's a silence around the table at the mention of Gran, but Declan quickly covers it by giving Cam his blessing to destroy the door if needs be.

"Will it work?" Cam looks at me doubtfully.

"It will either work or scare the crap out of her," I chuckle in response.

Cam stays with us a little longer, and once Declan has finished reassuring him that he'll be okay, he takes his leave of us to return to the farm.

As we wave Cam off from the car park Declan seems to sag a little. It's been a hell of a long day for him, and traumatic as hell. I take his arm and guide him back to the hotel. The hotel room looks no different to when I left it this morning, it feels wrong when so much has happened. I turn to Declan and ask him what he needs.

"Right now, a hot shower, then to curl up in bed with my woman," he responds.

"Want me to join you in the shower?" I offer. He nods his head in agreement. I know this isn't going to be our usual shower where we can't keep our hands off each other. Right now, what my man needs is to know I am there for him.

Once we're in the shower I slowly wash his body down, taking my time and being as gentle as I can. I hold him as he cries beneath the flow of hot water, and when he stops I dry him off with a towel and lead him to the bed. He curls up under the cover and looks so lost and lonely. I crawl in beside him, and he draws me in close. I'm expecting that tonight will bring back the nightmares he's been plagued by, but I'm wrong. I'm not sure if it's being in bed with me that keeps them at bay, or if he's just too exhausted to dream, but I'm relieved that he has what appears to be a restful night's sleep.

Cam

I'm exhausted by the time I pull up outside the farmhouse. Dawn has broken, and I can see Fred waiting on the porch for me. I take the steps slowly, not looking forward to being the bearer of bad news, but I don't have to say anything. He can tell.

"Ahh, it's a shame, she was a grand old lady," he sighs. "Leave it with me and I'll let everyone know. How's Declan?"

I let him know that Declan's about as good as could be expected right now. Fred bids me a good morning and sets off to deliver the news, his steps dragging as he goes.

Sahara is in the kitchen when I walk in, I don't know how she knows, but she does. She puts her arms around me and hugs me tightly. Its then that I allow myself to cry, I'm going to miss that amazing old lady. She was a bigger part of my life than I realized.

Sahara offers me a coffee, but I decline. I tell her that I'm too tired and she seems to understand. "Come on, let's get you to bed. You need to try and get some sleep." I follow her up the stairs, surprised when she opens the door to her room and pulls me in. She undresses me slowly, there's nothing sexual about it, just a friend helping a friend. She pulls the covers back and guides me to the bed before undressing herself and climbing in beside me. She opens her arms and I crawl into her embrace. I feel safe there. Nothing has been resolved between us, but I fall asleep in her arms, knowing that if I'd been on my own sleep would have eluded me. She fits me like a glove and I need to make things right between us.

Sahara

Cam falls asleep in my arms, and I ache for him, I want to take away the pain that he's feeling, I would if I could. I don't care what he's said, there's no way I'm not going to fight for this man. I'm going to give it my best shot, and if that fails, then at least I'll have tried. But that's going to have to wait, tonight I'm just going to hold him, let him know that I'm there for him. It's all I can do.

30

Declan

The last few days seem to have passed in a blur. There were meetings with the funeral director, the minister, phone calls to be made to distant relatives and friends to let them know about the funeral arrangements. It all felt surreal, I think I'm in denial that any of this is real. Through it all Holly has been by my side, keeping me strong. I don't know if I could have got through this without her. As much as I'm struggling I've not felt the need to lose myself in a bottle of JD, which has to be a good thing, although I think I'm going to need a shot or two to get me through today.

The mood in the house is somber, everyone dressed in black, ready for what the day will bring, our final goodbye to Gran. A part of me wants to run, to not be here to face this nightmare, but the part of me that Gran raised knows that's not an option. I owe it to her to be there for her today of all days.

The house feels empty without her presence, but everywhere I turn there's a memory. Her glasses on the arm of the chair, her needlepoint on the table unfinished. It's the sight of her apron in the kitchen that hits me the hardest. Some rooms look like she just stepped out, as if they're awaiting her return.

The caterer has arrived and is busy setting up, shooing us all out of the kitchen where we all seem to congregate. I'm wandering around the ground floor as though I'm lost, even though I grew up in this house, its seems unfamiliar to me now. I take the stairs and open the door to her room, taking a seat on the bed and hugging her pillow to me. I can still smell her. It's the first time I've been in here since I came back from the hospital, I couldn't face it before. It was Holly and Sahara who went in and picked out a dress for her to wear. The door creaks open and I look up, still hoping that Gran will walk in and it will all have been a horrible nightmare. Instead its Holly who comes in, sitting beside me quietly on the bed, leaving me to my memories.

"She's here," she finally whispers. "They're ready for you."

Holly holds my hand as I make my way out of the house where the hearse is waiting for us. There are so many people gathered here to pay their last respects. I take my place with Holly behind the hearse and we walk behind it to Gran's final resting place, next to Grandpa in a sheltered corner of the farm. She loved this spot, I'd often find her out here, kneeling at his graveside, telling him stories about what had been happening on the farm since her last visit.

The service itself seems to pass in a blur. The minister relating memories of this wonderful old lady that everyone is going to miss dreadfully. He nails it on the head, he knew her well. Too soon the moment comes for the coffin to be lowered. I stiffen my back, trying not to cry. Holly has a tight grip of my hand as her own tears fall, and Cam has his arm around my shoulder on my other side. The minister says his words of commitment then Sahara hands me a white lily to toss into the grave. They were Gran's favorite flowers. Hesitantly I step forward, kissing the petals of the flower before releasing it. "Goodnight, Gran. I love you." The sobbing around the grave gets louder as I let go of the lily, and one by one those closest to Gran step forward and say their own goodbyes.

The walk back to the house is somber, no one really knowing what to say. When we get to the house there are so many people wanting to offer condolences and share memories. It's a comfort to know how much she was loved.

The coffee and sandwiches soon make way for glasses of whisky, and the mood lightens as memories are shared. There are so many happy memories in this house, and I know that Gran had a good life.

It's almost eleven before the last guest leaves, Holly looks dead on her feet as does Sahara. I suggest we call it a night and the girls look at me with relief.

I'm staying in my room over the barn, I don't think I could have handled staying in the farmhouse.

"What are you going to do with the farm?" Holly asks me, she's already in bed and waiting for me to join her.

"I don't know, I haven't even thought about it." I haven't, and

I'm not sure what I want to do. I know I don't want to move back here and run the farm, it doesn't feel like home anymore, it's my bar back in Severed that is home now.

"I guess there's no rush," she offers, "I'm sure Fred will keep things running for you." She's right, I need to talk to Fred and find out what he wants to do. I've not just got myself to think about, there's everyone who relies on the farm for a living to consider.

Cam

I get into bed waiting for Sahara to join me and feel guilty that we still haven't spoken about our situation. The timing has been off. I need to let her know how I feel, but she's falling asleep on her feet, tonight isn't the time for our conversation. There's an unspoken truce at the moment. There's been nothing sexual between us since I returned from the hospital, but she shares her bed with me each night and always seems to be there when I need her during the day.

I look at my phone again, seeing the text from Greg. There's been a development and Jack Snr needs to meet with Declan and me. The jet is coming for us in the morning. I haven't told him yet, I'm not sure he's ready for this. If need be I can handle this without him, the guys are still here ready to move as soon as we make a decision.

Sahara walks in as I'm putting the phone back on the night-stand. She doesn't ask, but I tell her anyway. She seems to have a knack for helping me think things through. She's confident that Declan will be fine to go with me and thinks it will be good for him to get away from the farm for a few days. When I suggest that we'll be there and back in a day she disagrees.

"If Jack's called you to give you his blessing you need to be ready to act," she tells me. She's right, I hadn't thought of that. We need to be ready to move on the warehouse if we get the go ahead.

"What about you and Holly? I'm not comfortable leaving you here unprotected."

Sahara tuts away my comment, reminding me that Fred is more than capable of keeping an eye on things in my absence. Whilst she's right it still sits uneasy that I'll be away, and we don't know where Jerry is. I suggest leaving one of the guys behind and she discounts that idea as well.

"You work as a team, it won't be the same if one of you is missing." She's right about that as well. Every scenario we've considered has required the five of us working in tandem.

"We'll be fine," she reassures me. I just hope she's right.

31

Cam

*D*eclan wasn't happy about leaving the girls behind, but he agreed that they were safer here with Fred than being anywhere near Jerry's set up. It bothers us both that he seems to have gone to ground, but to be honest he's so lazy it's not like he'd do his own dirty work.

The guys are joking about the amount of time we're spending on Jack Snr's private jet, but they're not complaining at not having to travel economy. I have to say I could get used to this luxury. We'd sat down with Sahara the other night and are happy that we have a floorplan for the interior of the warehouse. It's always a risk entering a building which we haven't had first hand interior surveillance for, but it's not like we haven't done this plenty of times in the past. This is what we do.

We've discussed the options and our preferred plan is a night time assault in the early hours. From what we've seen most of the girls who are sent out to prostitute themselves nightly are normally back by one am. If we aim for something like half two in the morning we're hoping that the guards will be a little laxer than during the day. Jerry may think he runs an empire, but he's not the best when it comes to remunerating his employees which hopefully means that the guys working for him won't present us with too much of a challenge.

Greg wouldn't say what the development was, just that Jack Snr wanted to talk to me in person. I rack my brain trying to work out what it could be, but there are just too many scenarios to second guess, besides we'll be there in just over two hours and I'll find out then.

Declan isn't himself, not that I'm surprised. It's been a tough few days for him. He's not joining in the conversation, although he is sat watching Ryan take the mick out of Jacko's shirt. It's some floral thing that the girls probably wouldn't wear even. It's like water off a ducks back to Jacko and he takes the ribbing in good spirits. Luke's sitting quietly watching from the sidelines as he does. He's so quiet you often forget he's there, but he takes everything in, his intel is always spot on.

The flight passes quickly and without incident. That's the beauty of a private jet, it cuts down on so much faffing around. Greg is at the airport to greet us, he's brought two vehicles with him to accommodate us all.

He greets me with a slap on the back but goes to Declan and pulls him into a hug, offering his condolences. Looks like Greg is a bit of a gentle giant after all, still I wouldn't like to be on the wrong side of him.

Greg shows Declan and I into Jack's study and has one of his team take Jacko, Luke and Ryan to the kitchen for a coffee whilst they're waiting for us. Jack looks to have aged since I last saw him, something appears to have stressed him out.

"Cam, Declan," he greets us, shaking hands warmly. There's no mistaking his firm grip, this is a man who means business and it shows in his handshake unlike Jerry who has the limpest hand I've ever come across.

When we've taken the seats Jack gestures to, he gets down to business. He's reviewed the information that we sent over from our recon of the warehouse and he's satisfied that it is being used for trafficking. The photos lay scattered over the mahogany desktop and make for depressing viewing. Some of the girls shown can't even be sixteen. It makes my skin crawl to think of the future that awaits them if we don't do something.

"Even if Jerry wasn't involved I'd want this operation stopped," Jack sighs. "How did we not know this was happening under our noses." He's disappointed but he's not recriminating Greg, he's accepting equal responsibility.

"It's because Jerry is a low life scum bag, sorry boss, I know he's kin, but he's not worthy of the family name. I guess we all just let him get on with it, so we didn't have to actually spend time in his company." I understand what Greg is saying, there are some people, not many thankfully, that just sharing the same air as them makes your skin crawl. Jerry is one of them. There's this constant aura of unsavory around him that makes you want to spend as little time around him as possible. "The takings always added up, so it didn't look like there was any reason to dig deeper."

That's where Jerry has been clever, he's not skimmed money off the top, he's collected what he was asked to and handed it over. No reason to suspect him. No, instead he's set up his own illegal business that's raking in plenty of money.

"Do we know what kind of money he's turning over?" I'm naive and can't help the gasp that comes out when Greg tells me he's probably turning over in excess of a million a year through the warehouse. The girls that go out turning tricks nightly don't see any of the money they bring in, but they're not the money makers, that's the innocents like Sahara who are sold to order. Greg tells me that she had a price tag of a quarter of a million and that's why Jerry is so keen to get her back. I don't want to think about the kind of guy who would spend that much money to buy a woman, from everything Sahara told us they're the darkest and most perverted members of our society and their purchases rarely survive a few months of the sustained abuse and humiliation. What I do know is I'd like to get my hands on him and show him what I think of him.

The concern of all of us is what happens once we've taken down the warehouse. Is this business going to just pop up again somewhere else? The sad case is that it will, but it's a case of not in our back yard. We just have to accept that this is the best we are going to be able to achieve. If there's paperwork in the warehouse that leads back to the buyers then we can ensure that it anonymously arrives with the authorities, but that's not a priority.

Jack reassures us that he's satisfied it's Jerry behind the warehouse and business and we have his blessing to move forward. He reiterates though that when we're done Jerry has to disappear - permanently. He doesn't want to know anything about that element of our plan, just that its done. That way he doesn't have to lie to his sister when he tells her he doesn't know where Jerry is. That's fair enough, we don't have a problem with that.

Greg still hasn't found out where Jerry is, and Declan offers to contact Chris, see if he can track him through his credit card. We all agree it's the only option. It would be better for us if we knew where he is before we hit the warehouse so agree to wait a couple of days. I hate the thought of those girls having to suffer a day longer, but we'll have eyes on the warehouse in between. Right now, there isn't a better solution that we can think of. At least it means that in just a few days they'll be in a much safer place. Jack has found a local women's refuge to take them in. They'll be well looked after once we get them out of there.

All we can do now is wait. I hate waiting.

32

Cam

*A*fter the journey to Severed on the bike, and the past few weeks I'm tired of waking up in a hotel room. There's nothing wrong with this one, but I'm starting to feel like I want to live in one place, put down roots, have a home.

The other side of the bed is cold and unruffled. It feels wrong waking up on my own, I guess I've kind of got used to sharing with Sahara. I miss the warmth of her body next to me, the gentle rise and fall of her chest when she's restfully sleeping and the touch of her skin against mine.

I give myself a shake, I'm turning into a bloody old woman!

The phone rings and I reach over to the nightstand for it, it's the farm. I answer without thinking. "Morning Fred, how's it going?"

"It's not Fred, it's me." Sahara sounds a little put out that I'd assume it was Fred I guess.

"Oh, sorry. Morning. How's you?" I sit up against the pillows, running a hand through my hair. I hope everything's okay back there.

"Missing you," she confesses. "I couldn't sleep properly last night without you here."

I know how she feels, it was the same for me, but I'm not going to tell her that.

"Well, when I get back we'll go apartment hunting for you in Harvey if you want, sooner you have your own place the quicker you can get back to normal, unless you want to be somewhere busier like Perth?" There's a sigh from the other end of the phone followed by silence. I'm guessing that idea didn't go down too well.

"For me, or for us?" she finally responds, her words slow and measured.

"For you," I pause, trying to work out how to say it without hurting her too much. " I've told you, I can't do relationships. Look, I don't want to talk about this now, it's not the time or the place for it." I may have sounded a little harsh with that comment and brace myself for the retort I just know is going to come.

"Bullshit, Cam." There it is. "With you there's never going to be a time and a place to have this conversation because you keep avoiding it, and don't you dare hang up on me!" She's read my mind, I was about to end the call and claim loss of signal. Shit.

"Look, you and I both know there's something there between us, aside from the hot as fuck sex."

She's right, the sex is definitely hot, I smirk to myself.

"I think it's something worth following through on, you can't know if you won't even try."

"I'm too old for you, Sahara." The age gap bothers me, I'm a good twelve years her senior, granted not old enough to be her father, but certainly a much older brother. Before I can carry on with my excuses she interrupts me again.

"Bollocks," she hisses down the phone line. "You're just looking for bloody excuses now. Age doesn't matter here, Cam. We fit well together, you know we do."

"But...we're always fighting..." She cuts me off again.

"This is real life, Cam. People fight, people make up, they get on and live their lives full of passion and love. You think Fred and Edie don't fight? You should hear them at times, they have a right old session, especially if he gets in her way in the kitchen, but you know what, they talk it through, they apologize to each other and they make it up before they go to bed at night. That's how come they've lasted almost forty years, because they found something worth fighting for and didn't run at the first sign it might be tricky. I thought you were supposed to be special forces!" Her voice has risen throughout her rant and she almost screeches that last bit at me. Low blow, Sahara, low blow.

"I am... I was... I..." I've no idea what to say to her right now. God, give me an armed insurgent any day over an angry woman. I'm out of my depth here.

"Am I not worth fighting for, Cam?" There's such pain in that question it makes me feel like a total shit.

"You are, Sahara, you know you are, but like I've told you, you can do better than me, you deserve better than me."

"But that's the thing, Cam," she responds. "I don't want better than you, I want you. I don't think there's a better than you out there, not for me. You're it for me."

There's a silence from both ends of the phone, she's waiting for a response and I just don't know what to say.

"You remember that movie I made you watch, Notting Hill?" she eventually breaks the silence.

"Yeah?" It was cheesy as fuck, but it made me laugh. I'm not sure where she's going with this.

"Well, right now I feel like Julia Roberts, standing in that book shop, baring her soul to Hugh Grant and asking him to love her." She sighs again. "Don't make the mistake he did, Cam. Don't let me go."

That's deep shit she's throwing at me, and over the phone as well. My head's a shed of confused emotions here. "You mean I can't turn up at a press conference when I realize my mistake and claim to be from Horse and Hounds?" I joke. From the hiss that comes down the phone line I'm guessing that wasn't the mood lightening moment I was hoping for.

"Don't be a dick and joke about this, it's too important, well to me anyway."

"So, where do you want to go apartment hunting?" I try and

steer the conversation in a direction I'm more comfortable with.

"I don't," her reply is short and abrupt. "I don't want to leave here, it's just feels so much like home." She draws in a deep breath. I know how she feels, there's a peace at the farm I haven't found anywhere else. "I know that's not possible, I guess Declan will move back here, but I love being here."

I hadn't thought about Declan moving home. We haven't spoken yet about what he wants to do, he's only just got himself set up in Severed and I know, that despite all the trouble we had there, it's his sanctuary now from all the shit that happened in Afghanistan.

"I guess Harvey would be a better bet for you then," I suggest. "It's close by, has a tight community and you'd probably still be able to keep in touch with Fred and Edie if you wanted. You'd probably find Perth too busy and commercial for you."

"Yeah, probably." she pauses again. I hate these gaps in the conversation, I know what she wants me to say, but I can't bring myself to change, I'm not that man, not even for her.

"You don't have to decide anything right now," I try and reassure her. "There's no immediate plans for anything, nothing's changing until we have this Jerry situation sorted out."

"And then what?" I can't answer that for her, as much as she wants me to.

"I don't know," I respond honestly. "Look, I miss you in my bed, I miss your face, your smile and even you telling me off," I laugh. "We'll talk when I get back."

"You promise?" I hate the hint of hope that I can hear in

her voice.

"I promise."

I end the call, feeling like a total shit. Yeah, we'll talk when I get back, but I'm pretty sure it won't be the words that she's wanting to hear from me.

33

Cam

Chris called this morning and it turns out Jerry has taken a commercial flight to Thailand. Guess he's either gone on a buying trip for new girls, or he's selling. It makes sense, it's the human trafficking capital of the world. Either way it means he's out of our hair and the attack on the warehouse has the go ahead for tonight.

I thought about ringing Fred and giving him an update, so he could tell the girls, but then decided that they'd probably end up worrying unnecessarily. I'm going to ring him in the morning when it's all over, it's better that way.

I tried to nap this afternoon, so I'm rested for the mission, but I couldn't stop thinking about Sahara and all the reasons why she says we should give us a try. I need to clear my head of her so set about re-checking my kit for the sixth time.

Greg is coming with us tonight along with a couple of his most trusted team members. They've all seen action so we're confident that they'll be an asset rather than a hindrance unlike some of the Carnal bikers back in Severed. I hate working with amateurs.

We've pulled everything together that we need. We're not going in heavily loaded as its more about stealth, so there are knives and smoke bombs as well as some small firearms. The plan is in and out in as little time as possible. The location is remote enough we should hopefully avoid nosy neighbors.

We're going in at 2am and the clock seems to torment me with how slowly it's been moving. This is always the worst time, just before a mission. The anticipation builds, and you just want to get on with it.

We've spent the afternoon prepping the vehicles, we needed to black out a couple of minibuses for the girls, so we can take them to the refuge, Jack's been in contact and they'll be ready for us when we get there. They've arranged for a Doctor to be on site just in case. There's no telling what state some of the girls will be in, and they'll undoubtedly be too scared to go anywhere near a hospital or the authorities for a while. Sahara said some of the girls are international, they'd been promised a new life and job here and then had their passports confiscated and their families threatened if they didn't do what they were told when they got here. One of the girl's parents had actually paid the traffickers to take her, believing they were handing over their life savings to give her a good start in life. I don't think they could have imagined what that turned out to be, even in their worst nightmares.

There's finally a knock at the door to alert me that it's happening. Checking over my kit one last time I stand there for a moment, getting my head into the zone. I'm ready for this, bring it on.

☙

There's a weak light near the outside door of the warehouse, but no other security lighting and the exterior fence poses no challenge, its meant to stop the girls getting out, but a few quick snips and we've made a hole large enough for us to crawl through. We'll be leaving via the main gate when we're done to make it easier for the girls.

The two guards on duty are smoking and chatting to each other, they're not paying attention to the perimeter. They're sloppy and it's going to cost them. One throws his butt away and wanders off to the corner where he regularly relieves himself. A few hand signals to the team and both men are down. Silent and swift. They won't be getting back up as their throats have been cut from behind.

Our intel suggests that there were ten guards in all. Two down, eight to go. How convenient that there are eight of us. One a piece. Nice and easy.

The door is locked but the keys are on the belt of one of the heavies on the ground. Making sure everyone is in position I open the door lock and slowly ease the door, with it being a warehouse it opens outwards making it easier for us to slip in.

The interior is in darkness, there's an office off to one side where I can see the light of a flickering tv screen and hear laughter. With any luck most of the guards are slacking off in there.

As my eyes adjust to the gloom I count at least twenty beds in here. Not all of them are occupied, but the ones that are reveal slim figures huddled beneath rough blankets. It's a bit of a misnomer to call them beds, they're more like camp beds. For the money that Jerry is raking in, he certainly hasn't spared any of it making his merchandise comfortable.

We spread out around the room, Ryan, Greg and his team quietly rousing the girls and leading them outside where Jacko is waiting. Luke is out back, watching the rear exit and Declan and I are taking the office. We'll wait until the girls are out and the others can come back and join us before we make a move on it.

Jerry's thriftiness has played into our hands, he's not paying these guys enough to make them care about doing their job properly.

Ryan eases over and whispers in my ear that one of the girls is missing, I indicate the bathroom, I'm pretty sure from the noises coming from it one of the guards is in there getting a blow job. Nodding his understanding he moves over and goes in, there's a quiet pop from his silencer and then he comes out with a frightened blood-spattered teenager, holding his hand over her mouth to muffle the crying.

Greg moves behind me and assures me everyone is accounted for. It's time.

The office set up means that they're a captive audience, it's no fight really. I stroll in casually first, giving the impression

I'm alone. There's a clatter of chairs as they realize I'm there and start to move.

A few 'what the fucks' and its soon over. No one is left behind to talk.

Once the bodies have been removed Declan and I scan the office for anything useful.

"What the fuck!" he exclaims as he jimmies open one of the desk drawers. It's full of passports. The whole operation is so amateur it's a joke, he doesn't even have a safe. There's a laptop open on the desk and we take it with us. We'll send it to Chris and hopefully he can find some information about buyers on there that will prove useful to the authorities. Looking at the way this place has been set up I doubt there's even a password on there.

When we go outside the lock on the gate has been cut off and the minibuses have been pulled in. The girls are huddled in blankets and have the same numb expression on their faces that Sahara did when I first met her.

We've done a good thing tonight, but I'm under no illusion that this is a drop in the ocean. The buyers will just go elsewhere to source their illicit requirements, the sellers will find another mug like Jerry. It's a massive industry that grows daily.

Once we've made sure the girls are safe at the refuge we call it a night. Greg has arranged to leave a couple of guys close by just in case, but we're done for now.

I want to get back to the farm, let Sahara know everything's fine, but more than that I want to find Jerry. What he did to her was bad enough but having seen how young some of these girls were tonight I'm even more determined to find the fucker and finish him.

You're mine Jerry, you're mine.

34

Sahara

*H*olly had walked into the kitchen as I ended my call with Cam yesterday morning. She'd taken one look at my face and decided we needed a shopping trip to cheer us up. I know I was tired of washing the limited clothes I have every few days, it was worse than trying to live out of a suitcase in a way and agreed.

Fred spoiled our retail therapy idea as he said he couldn't leave the farm, he'd already got plans for the day but promised to juggle things around, so he could come with us today instead. He hadn't liked Holly's suggestion that she was more than capable of driving us and we didn't need a bodyguard. He'd promised Declan he'd take care of us and that was that.

A compromise was reached, Fred and Edie would go with us as she'd got some shopping she wanted that she couldn't get locally, and they'd give us space as long as we were always in their line of sight. Holly reluctantly agreed.

Walking around the mall with Holly, closely, but not too closely followed by Fred and Edie made me chuckle. I felt like a pre-teen being followed by her parents on her first solo venture into the big wide world. I suspect Holly had a very different upbringing to me, she doesn't have memories like that. I guess when it was just her and her brother she grew up more quickly than a child should have had to. That probably explains her strength and that stubborn streak I am sure is going to get her into trouble one day. I think that's why she and Declan get on so well, she's not some weak helpless female, she stands up to him. I wonder how Cam sees me? I'm no Holly for sure. I reckon he thinks I'm some fragile princess who needs locking up in a tower, except in this fairy tale she won't be getting her prince.

Holly jars me out of my daydream by suggesting we stop for coffee. She sneaks a peak behind us, Fred's not looking very enamored by the noise and crush in the mall, so she tells him we're having a break for his benefit. Fred meanwhile looks at the 5″ heels Holly insisted on wearing and offers the opinion the coffee break is less for his well-being and more to rest her feet from those monsters she's wearing. He could be right, there's no way I could walk round a shopping mall in those things.

"Look, I've had to wear sensible footwear on the farm, it's about time I got to wear my pretties." She smiles as she lifts her foot, turning it this way and that to admire the shoes.

Fred and Edie sit a few tables away from us, but somewhere that he can still see us and watch the doorway. Part of me feels like I have a jailer, but the little girl in me is reassured that someone is there, watching my back. It feels like a long time since I had that.

Holly is picking chunks of her blueberry muffin and placing them in her mouth when she suddenly remembers something.

"I know what I wanted to ask you!" She almost chokes on that last bit of muffin, but recovers quickly, easing it down with a sip of the hot coffee. "Whatever happened to Tom?"

When I'd told Holly my story I'd ended the part with Tom at the hospital when his mother threw me out, partly because that's where my life with Tom ended, but also because what came next is a painful recollection. I take a drink of coffee, bracing myself, the memories flooding back.

"You remember his mother threw me out of the hospital? Well, it was well over a year before I found out what happened next, I bumped into Chas one day in the supermarket. It was only mid-day, but he was already drunk. That driver didn't just destroy mine and Tom's lives that day, he destroyed Chas's as well. The guilt ate away at him until the only place he could find solace was in a bottle.

Chas offered to take me for a drink so we could catch up, and I agreed as long as it was coffee. You should have seen the look of disgust on his face, but he agreed as he had something he wanted to tell me.

Chas began by apologizing to me, and at first, I couldn't understand why, he was blaming himself for everything that had happened and kept saying it was all his fault. Then he explained.

That night at the campout Chas had put something in my

drink, it was only supposed to be a joke, a bit of fun he'd said. He never guessed what repercussions would come from that one small act. If he'd not done that, I'd never have got pregnant, Tom wouldn't have been going to see his parents that day, and he'd never have been knocked from his bike by the drunk driver.

I tried to console him by showing him a photo of Sophia that I kept in my purse, if he hadn't done what he did then I wouldn't have had my angel. He smiled when he saw her face and commented that she had Tom's eyes. She did. Every time I looked at my baby I saw Tom, the Tom I loved, not the Tom I still remembered from the hospital.

I hesitantly asked how Tom was, it hadn't come up in the conversation so far. Chas's face fell instantly, and I could tell it wasn't going to be good news.

Tom's helmet had been knocked off in the crash and left him with serious head injuries. The night I'd been chased off by his mother they'd had to do an operation to remove part of his skull to relieve the pressure. Chas commented that from the front you wouldn't be able to tell, but when you sat at the side of him, it was the weirdest thing, his forehead was concave, although the skin there was unmarked once the scratches and bruises faded. His mother used to make him wear a baseball hat when she visited. When he finally came around from his coma the brain injury was too devastating. There was no way he was going to be able to walk again, his speech was massively limited and his vision impaired. With brain injuries like this a person's behavior changes and Tom's was challenging to say the least. He'd lash out and hit anyone who came near him to try and help him. He didn't know where he was, or why, he just couldn't understand that, but he did know that he should be doing things for himself like eating and washing, so when someone had to help him because he couldn't do it himself he became violent.

He'd been moved to a brain injury rehab hospital that specialized in patients with this kind of challenging behavior, Chas assured me it was the best care money could buy, but sadly it hadn't been enough. A few months after arriving there Tom caught an infection and passed away in his sleep.

I sat there in shock, Tom was gone. I'd not expected that. I think I honestly believed he'd recover and go back to being the man his parents wanted him to be. At least this explained the lack of contact from him, I couldn't believe he wouldn't want to see his daughter.

Chas kept telling me that it was a blessing really, that there'd have been no quality of life for him. Then he started apologizing again. He kept going back to that pill at the campout, and how that one action had destroyed so many lives."

Holly has sat there silently the whole way through my story, the look of shock on her face obvious. I don't think I've ever seen Holly lost for words before.

She excuses herself to go to the bathroom, and I see Edie get up and discreetly follow her whilst Fred keeps his eyes on me.

Meanwhile I take another sip of my coffee and think that it wasn't the pill that caused all this, it was that turn of the card.

35

Declan

*I*t was four am before we got back to the hotel, but I just wanted to get home to Holly, I'd rather sleep back at the farm with her than in this anonymous room. Cam was in agreement, so Greg kindly sorted out the jet for us again.

"We should get frequent flyer miles for the amount of time we've spent on this jet," Jacko jokes once we're on board. Ryan flicks a peanut at his head in response. The late night hasn't affected them either, we're all still high on adrenalin.

The flight is as smooth as always and I manage to doze on and off until we land. When I turn my phone on there's a missed call and a text from Holly telling me she's going to the mall with Sahara, but not to worry they'll have Fred with them.

The trucks we left are still parked at the airport, I suggest the guys go back to the farm whilst Cam and I head to the mall to meet the girls. I don't know what's happening between him and Sahara, but I sure as hell want to hold Holly in my arms as soon as possible.

We've not reached the truck when my phone rings with Holly's number again.

"Hey, babe, I missed you," I start to say before I'm interrupted by a hysterical Sahara. I can barely make out what she's saying between her sobs. "Slow down, say that again, I didn't catch it."

"It's Holly!" she screams down the phone. "They've taken her..."

Cam's driving as I'm not in a fit state. He had to take the phone off me as I'd started shouting at Sahara, it's not her fault, but there was no one else to blame. It's down to me, I shouldn't have left Holly, I should have been protecting her. I didn't want her to come on this trip, but the stubborn arse refused to stay behind. God, if anything's happened to her I don't think I can handle it.

Cam's on the phone with Chris seeing if he's got any intel that can help us.

Whoever grabbed Holly did it quickly and without fuss. One minute she was chatting to Sahara, the next she'd gone to the bathroom and not come back, her handbag still on the floor where she'd been having coffee. She doesn't even have the bloody gun with her to protect herself. Shit! The phone was left behind in the bag, so we can't use that to track her.

The mall is only ten minute's drive from the airport, but it feels like hours. At the time it seemed like a good idea to keep the girls out of harms reach at the farm. Yeah, hindsight is telling me it wasn't such a great idea now.

Cam persuaded Sahara not to call the police and to wait for us in the coffee shop. She looks a mess when we walk in. Tears stain her cheeks and she's wringing her hands in despair. God knows what the waiting staff are making of it all. Fred is standing beside her, ashen faced. When Edie hadn't come back from the bathroom either he'd asked Sahara to go in and check on them. Edie was on the floor, unconscious and blood from a head wound pooling on the floor.

As soon as Sahara sees Cam she jumps up and runs to him. He pulls her in close as she breaks down. I can barely hear what she's saying, just the odd apology and how it was all her fault. Putting my hand on her shoulder I smile at her and tell her it wasn't.

"It's nothing you could have prevented," I reassure her. "This is on me. I should have had a better plan to keep you two safe."

Persuading her back to the seat of the booth she slowly calms down enough to tell us what had happened. They'd been chatting over coffee when Holly had needed to go to the bathroom, Edie had followed her but neither came out. When Sahara had gone to investigate at Fred's request there was no sign of Holly and Edie was out cold. Fred looks sick.

"How's Edie?" Cam asks, looking around the room. "Where

is she?"

"They took her to the hospital, I told them I'd follow as soon as you guys got here, I couldn't leave her on her own," he gestures to Sahara. He looks so torn, he wants to keep Sahara safe, but you can tell he wants to be with his wife. Cam thanks him for staying but tells him we've got it from here, he should get to the hospital and make sure Edie is okay.

"Did anyone call the police?" I ask.

"No, we knew you wouldn't want us to," Fred responds. "They think Edie had a slip on the floor and accepted my explanation when I said I needed to wait for you guys to get here as I couldn't leave Sahara on her own, she was in shock at finding her."

"How did they get her out?" I look at the coffee shop, unable to work out how they could have got Holly out when Fred was watching the door. He looks embarassed.

"As Edie had gone in with her I was watching Sahara," he confesses. "They must have taken her out of the back." He points to the service entrance that leads to the rear of the mall. It's at the end of the corridor where the bathroom is located and as that's all that's down there and it's a shady corridor it's not a door that would have been observed by the rest of the customers.

Looking out at the busy mall I can't believe they had the opportunity. It's heaving with people right now. How the hell did they find the girls? How are they keeping up with us? Where the fuck have they taken Holly? I swear if they hurt one hair on my girl's head there will be hell to pay. I'll unleash Armageddon on them.

"Why did they take Holly instead of me?" Sahara is still distraught.

"I'm guessing she was the easier target." Cam tries to calm her down, his hand rubbing slowly on her back.

"What happens now?" She asks. Good question.

"If Jerry can track the girls to here, I'm sure he'll find a way to get a message to us."

Cam suggests. "You think he'll want to swap?"

Sahara pales at the mention of a swap.

"Don't worry, honey, we're not going to let him get you," he promises her. "We're just hoping he'll think we'll consider it. At least that way we'll have a rough idea where he is."

"Bastard!" I slam my hand down too hard onto the table, earning a glare from the waitress who's been watching us since we got here.

"I don't think there's any point staying here, Declan," Cam suggests. "We need all the help we can get on this one, let's get back to the farm and the guys. I'll call Chris."

He starts to leave the booth and Sahara grips hold of his hand, she doesn't want him to go. "It's okay, Declan's going to watch out for you. I'm just going to make a few calls and get some help."

Sahara slowly releases her grasp, looking at me for reassurance. "I'm here don't worry." Her hand is on the table, so I reach over to pat it. "We're going to sort this out, and when we're done, Jerry isn't going to be able to hurt anyone ever again. I promise you."

Right now, I have no idea how we're going to find Jerry, but one thing I am sure of, he's mine and he's going to pay for taking my girl.

36

Holly

The room they've put me in is decrepit; it looks like an abandoned house. For all its shabbiness it's solidly built, I know, I've tried every way I can think of to open the door or get the boards off the window.

There's nothing in here to help me. I'm cuffed by one wrist to a metal bedstead, that's still got too much life in for me to break it. I left my bag back under the table in the coffee shop at the mall so I've no weapon either. Some girl scout I am. I don't even have a nail file on me.

The room smells of stale piss and rotten food. I'm sure I heard something scuttling about in the dark corner, just what I need, rats or vermin on top of this.

The guys who took me aren't the smartest tools in the box. I know their names for a start, Brad and Jim. Amateurs. I don't think they're used to being hired muscle, they may have got me out of the mall, but they left Sahara behind. My brother Justice always made sure I could look after myself if needed. Kneeing one attacker, Brad, in the balls was so easy, although he does have a pretty good backhand. What did he expect for hitting an old lady! I think I may have a bruise on my face from the blow he gave me when he got over the shock of my assault. I can't believe they were waiting in the bathroom for me, I just hope Edie's alright, that was a hell of a smack to the head they knocked her out with.

Whoever got them to take me has obviously told them not to hurt me, Jim told him off for hitting me. That's a good sign, I think.

Jim's the older of the two, he also seems the most self-assured. He told me that if I behave myself I'll be fine. They don't want to hurt me.

It was the way that Brad sniggered about not damaging the merchandise that unnerved me. If these guys work for Jerry as I suspect, then my future's not looking rosy.

I can't hear anyone else, I tried quietly tapping on the wall, but there was no response. The only noise is the drone of a television in the room at the front of the house where I'm guessing Brad and Jim are hanging out. I haven't even heard a phone ring. If I could get out of this room I'm not sure where I'd go, I had a blindfold on in the car and couldn't hear anything that gave me a clue which direction we'd gone in. Even the ring of a phone would have given me hope that I could call for help if I got out of the room.

Hopefully by now Declan will know that I've gone. He'll

come up with a plan. I'm sure of it. The door creaks open and I wonder what fresh hell awaits me now.

I just need to stay calm and wait for my Wounded Heroes.

Declan

I've been pacing the floor of the farmhouse for what feels like forever. The lock screen of my phone is taunting me, I just want it to ring. Surely if they have her then they'll be in touch to arrange a ransom or a swap.

Cam's on the phone with Chris and pacing just as much as me. There's a few too many fucks in his conversation but I can't hear the other side of it so am just going to have to wait for the call to end to find out what it's about.

On a mission I can sit for hours, not moving, just biding my time waiting for the perfect moment to strike. This isn't a mission though and this isn't some nameless stranger involved, this is my girl. I try sitting on the sofa, but my foot has a nervous tap that's driving me insane, so I stand up again.

I double check the phone screen to make sure I have a signal, but its good. I'd throw it in frustration but know I can't. It could be the only lifeline I have to getting Holly back.

Cam finally finishes on the phone and comes over. He looks pissed off.

"That was Chris," he starts.

"I gathered that," I can't help snapping back at him. "What did he say?"

Cam ignores my rudeness. "His intel was wrong. Jerry bought the plane ticket to Thailand, but he never boarded the plan. His operative failed to follow through on the lead. He's finally found him on the CCTV at the airport we just came from. Jerry's here."

I know Chris well, he'll be furious that his operative fucked up. We never would have carried out the raid on the ware-house last night if we'd known he was this close to the girls. We'd have dealt with him first. I choose not to think what Chris will do, but at the least I'm guessing that guy won't be staying employed past the end of this morning.

Jacko, Luke and Ryan come back in, they've been out checking the perimeter of the farm, looking for anything suspicious. Ryan shakes his head, they've found nothing. I doubt they'll have taken Holly too far away. Chris is scanning satellite images to see if he can find anything that will help us find where they've taken her.

We've been back two hours when Fred returns, an ashen faced Edie in tow.

"I'm so sorry, Declan," I couldn't get out to warn Fred. I rush over to her and pull her into a hug, reassuring her. It's not her fault. There's only one person at fault here and that's Jerry.

"She shouldn't be here," Fred looks at his wife warmly, "they wanted to keep her in, check for concussion, but she insisted on coming back here and helping." A look passes between them that's so full of love.

Luke sits down with Edie and spends the next half hour getting as much detail from her as she can remember about the kidnappers. Despite the blow to the head she remembers enough detail that Luke can draw a sketch of them.

"That's them!" She gasps. That one there is the one who hit me. The younger one."

For an old lady who's had a traumatic morning she's done a great job and has given us something to send to Chris to see if he can match names to faces. It's all going to take time though, and this waiting is killing me. I want to be out there, smashing heads, getting answers and rescuing my woman.

Edie insists on making us lunch, even though no one's hungry. Cam tries to reason with her and tell her to go rest. Fred just shrugs his shoulders and tells us to let her get on with it. Keeping busy is her way of coping, not to mention she's feeling responsible for not being able to stop the kidnapping.

If guilt was a physical thing you could cut it with a knife in this room, the air is full of it.

Cam's phone rings and we all jump, he looks at the number on the screen and shakes his head. It's Greg calling to let us know that the girls we rescued last night are all going to be fine physically, although some of them have a long road ahead and will need a lot of counselling. At least something good came from last night.

It's another hour before a message comes through on my phone from an unknown number. I almost drop it when I see the accompanying picture message.

Holly is tied to a chair, a hand covering her mouth so all I can see is the fear in her eyes. You can't see the face of the guy standing behind her, but you can see the huge knife being held against her throat.

There are just four words in the accompanying message: I WANT WHAT"S MINE

37

Cam

*D*eclan's phone just beeped with an incoming message and judging by the look of horror on his face, Jerry's made contact. We all rush over to see what the message says, Edie gets there before me and breaks down in tears. Fuck, what can it be? Fred has to take her out of the room as she's growing hysterical.

When I see the image, I thank fuck Sahara's upstairs, Jacko had to give her a sedative earlier as she wouldn't stop crying. Seeing that image of Holly with a knife to her throat would have killed her.

I'm confused by Jerry's message as he hasn't given us any instructions, then again this is Jerry, he's probably enjoying messing with us. Does he know about the warehouse last night? Is that why the snatch happened this morning? So many questions running through my head right now and we don't have the answers to any of them.

There's nothing in the photo to give us a clue to where they're holding Holly. The lack of information along with the fear that the photo has instilled in all of us makes it hard to just sit back and wait. We can't go off halfcocked here, as much as we hate it we just have to wait for something to happen.

Declan is pacing the room, swearing every time he looks at the image on his phone. I feel useless. It's best just to leave him to it right now.

My phone vibrates in my pocket and I'm relieved to see Chris's name on the screen, I just hope he has some intel for us.

"I've found him!" Chris's voice, normally so calm, holds a hint of excitement. "There's no sign that Holly is being held in the same location though, it looks like he's holed up in a hotel with just one of his cohorts."

"Yes!" I shout out, startling the rest of the room who turn to look at me with anticipation in their faces.

Chris is going to send over the location and some aerial surveillance shots he got from one of his drones. Those things have revolutionized recon in the past couple of years and were a godsend when we were checking out the warehouse.

I wake up my laptop and the images seem to take forever to come through. Declan doesn't recognize the hotel, but Fred does. The atmosphere in the room is electric now we finally have something to focus on. It's about half an hour away from us. There's nothing in the immediate vicinity that looks like it would be a good place to hold Holly, and Chris is adamant she's not at the hotel. He'd tapped into the

CCTV and been able to tell us that Jerry had been there all morning, before Holly was snatched.

"So, what do you want us to do?" I look at Declan. He's always been our leader, despite how he feels about what happened in Afghanistan he's never let us down. There's no one else I would trust more.

"We take Jerry," his voice is calm and controlled, he's back in the zone. "From what Chris has told us he's not well guarded, and once we have him, we make him tell us where Holly is."

Declan looks around the room, considering. "Cam, you come with me. The rest of you, be ready to move when we give you the call, they could be holding Holly anywhere, so we need to spread out, so we can get there quickly when we know the location."

"What about me?" Fred asks.

"I need you to stay here and look after Sahara and Edie, that okay?" Declan tells him.

"Yes, sir, happy to oblige." Fred looks pleased to have some part to play in this, and it reassures me that someone I trust will be here for my girl. I just called Sahara my girl I realize. When this shit is over, I need to really think about what I want, now isn't the time for that though. I need to get my head back in the zone.

We agree that Declan and I will deal with Jerry, Jacko and Ryan will be in one vehicle ready to move and Luke will be in another. With his sniper skills he's better off working alone from a distance. As soon as we find out where Holly is being held we can move in together.

The drive to the hotel seems to last forever, I double and triple check the photos that Chris has sent through, making sure our entry plan is the right one. Jerry's in a room at the rear of the hotel which plays into our plan nicely. There's less chance of being observed back there. The plan is to get into his room, secure him and then question him. We'll deal with anyone who gets in the way, although from what we've been told there's only one hired hand with him. On paper it looks like a simple smash and enter, but you never know. It pays to have a contingency plan.

The hotel is middle of the road, part of a chain. There's a check in office off to the left, but we drive past it and round the back where we park up several doors away from Jerry's room. The cleaners store is close to where we park, and it takes no time to force the lock and gain entry. We both don anonymous beige overalls, and once we're armed with a cleaning trolley and a mop and bucket we don't look out of place. Slouching so we appear bored and disinterested, but mainly to hide our faces, we roll the cleaning gear along the path until we're outside Jerry's door.

The mop is hiding our faces if anyone were to look out of the peephole as we knock on the door, shouting out a disinterested sounding 'room service'. There's a mumbled 'not today' from behind the door. Ignoring it I use the master key I found in the cleaning store to unlock the door.

Before the heavy can shut the door on us, I've jammed it open with my foot, and use the element of surprise to slam it into him knocking him back enough for us to gain access.

He's not the smartest tool in the box, and his weight means he takes a moment to regain his balance, that's all I need.

Before Declan has the door secured the heavy lies immobile on the floor, my knife in his neck.

Jerry is on the bed, backing up to the headboard as if he can escape what's happening in front of him. I leave him to Declan, who's on him in a flash, his own knife just pricking the skin of his gross triple chin.

"Where is she?" Declan hisses.

"She's not here you stupid fuck," Jerry laughs in his face. "You've just signed her death warrant." Jerry has that fucking smirk on his face. Declan soon wipes it away though as he pushes the knife a little deeper, just enough to release a trace of blood.

"Let me make this simple for you, you fat fucker. Your life is over, you picked on the wrong people. Right now, you have a decision to make, I can kill you quickly or I can kill you slowly and believe me you really don't want the second option." Declan speaks with such calm authority even I feel a chill on my skin.

"Fuck you," Jerry spits in Declan's face. The spittle hits him on his cheek, and he brushes it away with the back of his free hand.

"Big mistake, Jerry, big mistake."

38

Holly

The door creaks open and I brace myself for what is to come. I can't imagine it will be anything good. I'm pleasantly surprised when I see it's Jim and he's holding a takeout bag in his hand. The aroma of grease hits my nostrils and I realize I'm hungry. I'm not sure how long I've been here, I think I was out of it earlier and without being able to see what time of day it is through the boarded-up window, it could be hours since I last ate.

Jim delivers the food in silence, leaving the room and locking the door behind him. I open the bag and my stomach rumbles in appreciation at the sight of the burger and fries inside. I want to take my time, make the moment last, but I find myself gobbling the food down, not sure when I'll get a meal again.

I'm so grateful for the diet soda but manage to ration that more sensibly. I hadn't been aware of how thirsty I was until

I took the first sip and wanted to gulp the drink down in one. I don't think the dirt in this room is helping, there are dust motes hovering in the air around me and it's so thick on the surface of the chest of drawers that I could write my name in it.

I want to pace the room, I'm feeling as frustrated as a caged animal, but the metal cuff restricts my movements. I'm slightly regretting my choice of footwear now, these heels are sexy as hell, but totally impractical for a quick getaway should the opportunity present itself. I'd take them off, but don't want to risk missing a chance.

The mattress springs creak as I try to move into a more comfortable position and shift my weight on it, I cringe at the stains that are visible. It's certainly seen some use and I don't really want to think what that use was, especially with the way Brad looked at me earlier. Considering the business that Jerry is in I can guess. My arm aches in this position, but it's the best I can do.

I've exhausted the opportunities for eye spy, and to be fair it's pretty boring when you're playing against yourself. I switch to counting the flowers on the faded wallpaper instead. That's only marginally more entertaining.

The drone of the TV outside is muted by the sound of raised voices. I can only pick out odd words. Brad is shouting at Jim about not hearing from Jerry, there's a hint of panic in his voice. Jim on the other hand remains calm, so calm I can't hear his responses. I wish he'd speak up. I'm not sure what this means for me, if they haven't heard from Jerry does that mean that Declan has found him, that he's on his way to rescue me?

I quell down the feeling of hope that the idea has raised. It's dangerous to think like that and might only lead to disappointment. If he is on his way to rescue me then I need to be ready.

The sound of the front door slamming startles me a little. Has someone left, has someone new come in? Please don't let it be Jim who's gone out, the thought of being left alone here with Brad raises my hackles. I don't like the way he leers at me, it's like he undresses me with his eyes. He makes me feel dirty.

There's no sound of conversation anymore so I guess it means one of them has gone. Surely if it was Jim then Brad would have been in here by now, I can't see him missing a chance to torment me.

My bladder is aching for release, as much as I enjoyed the diet soda it perhaps wasn't the best idea. Looking around the room I can't see anything that looks like it's been left for me to use, and there's no sign of a bathroom. I try not to think about my need to pee, but as is the way, I can't not think about it.

I'm left with no choice but to shout for my remaining captor. Please let it be Jim.

"Hey, I need to pee!" There's no response. Maybe they don't believe me, or maybe they've both gone out? I don't want to be left in this hell hole alone, and I really don't want to wet myself on this mattress. I start to panic, stamping my feet on the floor to make more noise and continuing my plea for the bathroom.

The click of the door lock silences me and I watch with a

mix of fear and hope as the door opens. I almost pee myself with relief when its Jim standing in front of me, not Brad.

"I'm sorry, I can't let you go to the bathroom till he gets back." Jim apologizes.

"But I'll pee myself!" I screech. "You're the one who brought me the bloody soda, what did you think was going to happen?" I rattle the cuff against the bedstead in frustration.

Jim looks sorry for me and I decide to play on the sympathy, begging and pleading for the use of the bathroom. "You can even leave the door open," I offer. He cocks his head to one side, considering whether he can trust me I guess. "Please!"

"Okay, okay, but no silly moves." Jeff may be the gentler of the two guards, but his voice leaves no doubt he won't put up with anything.

"I promise." I wiggle my legs, trying to relieve the burning need to pee, it's not working, if anything it makes it worse.

I'm so genuinely desperate for the bathroom that I don't do anything to jeopardize my chance, I'm grateful when he lets me push the door to, but not fully shut it, at least he's given me an element of privacy. I still feel like I'm being watched, and it seems to take an age before I can go, when I do it goes on forever.

"Hurry up in there," Jim huffs impatiently. "If Jerry finds out I've let you out he'll go mental."

"I'm going as fast as I can, it's not easy with you out there." I retort.

I finish as quickly as I can, running my hands under the cold tap to try and clean them, then having to dry them on my jeans when I see there's no towel. "I'm done." I call as I open the door.

Without the distraction of trying not to wet myself I take in everything I can on the walk back to the room. I can see a compact living room with a TV in the corner, a couple of windows and a solid looking front door. There's an open plan kitchen in one corner and a couple of doors aside from the bathroom that I assume both lead to bedrooms, one of them being the room I'm being held captive in. There's no road noise from outside, so I could be in the middle of nowhere. If I could get out where would I go?

Jim opens the door for me to return to my prison. If I'm going to do something I know I need to do it now. I may not get another chance. Keeping my head straight I look out of the corner of my eyes trying to find anything I can use as a weapon. There's nothing. My hands are free, with the cuffs dangling from one wrist, but they're no good to me. Suddenly it comes to me, there's only one thing I can use. I need to be quick and I need to be ready.

As I start to walk through the doorway I stumble on my heel and fall down. Jeff reaches down to help me off the floor, and that's his mistake. Grabbing the shoe that came off when I fell I turn on him, throwing every bit of strength I can into the blow. I cringe as the five-inch heel breaks through the skin on his neck, burying itself deep. Jim's hands grasp for the shoe, but the amount of blood he's losing leaves him with no strength. Grabbing for my shoe I yank it out and am covered by the arterial flow that gushes out. His eyes glaze over in death and he falls to the ground.

I stand there in shock, frozen. I just killed a man. I want to throw up, but I don't have time. I quickly replace my bloody shoe on my foot and rush for the front door. I'm so grateful to find it unlocked. I've no idea what is out there, what I'll be running into, but I don't have a choice. I just have to pray that Declan is out there somewhere, looking for me and finds me before Jerry does.

39

Cam

*W*e bundle Jerry into the back of the truck cab, we're taking him back to the farm, there's too much activity at the hotel to allow us to get information out of him. Chris has arranged for a cleanup crew to go in and take care of the room for us. He's proving to be a very useful ally.

Jerry made it clear he wasn't going to talk but doesn't realize how effective Declan and I are at interrogation. I'm going to enjoy torturing this fat fucker. He deserves everything he has coming to him.

Declan is in the back with Jerry, his .22 cocked and a look on his face that would scare the most hardened of soldiers. There's a smell of piss hovering around Jerry, once he realized how serious the situation was he lost control of his bladder. I try not to breathe through my nose as I drive, thankfully Jerry is gagged for the journey, so I have the driver's side window open wide, at least the warm air that's flowing in is fresh.

Declan's mobile rings, he manages to remove it from his pocket and unlock it without moving the gun aimed at Jerry.

"Holly!" His voice is full of shock. "Where are you? What happened? How did you get away?" He quick fires questions at the handset and I'm frustrated as hell that I can't hear the other half of the conversation.

"We'll be there, hang on baby, we're coming." Declan ends the call, a look of absolute shock on his face.

"What?" I throw back over my shoulder, trying to watch his face in the rear-view mirror whilst still giving my attention to the road ahead of me.

"Holly escaped," he laughs. "My girl escaped thanks to those bloody heels of hers." He sees the confusion on my face and promises to explain later. When he tells me where she's hiding I know we're too far away, Luke is closer to her location.

Declan objects when I say I'll send Luke to pick her up, he wants to go there now, but I remind him that she's safe, and we have a package that we need to deal with first. Declan's gaze drops to Jerry. He's heard every word we've said, and when he realized that Holly had escaped his face dropped into a mask of defeat and resignation.

"Yeah, we have some shit we need to take care of." Declan grins. "Call Luke, get him to take her back to the farm. Once I've seen my girl is okay, we'll deal with him," he nods at Jerry. "And if those fuckers hurt one hair on my girl's head, " he directs his words at Jerry now, "you'll understand the definition of pain," he promises him.

I call Luke and let him know Holly's location, he's only minutes away from her thankfully and assures me he'll get her back to the farm as quickly as he can. Declan rings the number that Holly had called from, apparently she'd found a mobile phone in an unlocked car outside the house she'd been held captive in. There weren't any car keys and she wasn't too keen on going back in the property to check over the guy she'd taken out. She was hiding in the bushes nearby, too blood soaked to venture further afield. He lets her know that Luke is on the way, and that we'll send Luke her number, so he can let her know when he's close. We don't want to risk the ring tone alerting anyone to her presence so advise her to set the phone to vibrate.

"What the hell?" I laugh when Declan ends the call. "I can't believe your girl escaped."

The relief and pride is overflowing in Declan's voice as he replies. "That's my girl, I knew she was a tough cookie, but I never saw that coming."

By the time we arrive at the farmhouse, Luke has already made it back. As soon as I move to relieve him from guarding our captive, Declan shoots up the steps to the porch where Holly is sat in a blanket on the swing. Edie is comforting her, but it's obvious from the way she's shaking that the shock has set in. As she sees Declan she stands quickly, the blanket falling away, and I gasp when I notice how much blood there is on her clothing. What has the poor girl been through?

Declan pulls her into his arms, and she breaks down, the trauma of what she's been through finally being released.

Calling Jacko and Ryan over I ask them to escort Jerry to his new accommodation. He looks relieved, he shouldn't. I've prepared the shed for him, and he's going to find it less than accommodating.

Jacko indicates at Declan and Holly, "Take your time, he's not going anywhere. We'll keep an eye on him, you two just make sure your girls are okay."

He's right, now Holly is safe there's no rush to deal with Jerry. As Declan had told him, there was an easy way, or a hard way. He's going to regret choosing the hard way as its going to be very long and drawn out, and incredibly painful. But first, we need to take care of our girls.

Jerry is crying as he's dragged off by the guys, offering to make peace. "I'm sure we can sort this out," he sobs.

"Oh, we'll sort this out alright," I look him straight in the eyes. "We'll sort this out once and for all," I assure him.

Looking around the porch I can't see Sahara. Edie comes over, placing her arm on mine, obviously sensing what I'm looking for. "She's in her room," she advises. "She got a little hysterical when she saw Holly so Jacko had to sedate her again," she shudders as she looks at Holly's bloodstained appearance, "not that I blame her."

Luke catches us up on the events at the house where Holly was held captive, he'd arrived at the same time the second kidnapper had returned and advises us that there are now two bodies to clean up there. I'll let Chris and his team know. "Holly says there were only two of them from start to finish, and they're both dealt with now." Luke confirms, looking at Holly with a touch of awe.

"Thanks, Luke, thank you for being there and bringing my girl back to me," Declan's voice sounds tired. "I think I need to let my girl get cleaned up now," he indicates Holly who has pretty much collapsed exhausted on him.

Declan is almost carrying Holly into the house, whispering promises of revenge in her ear, at the same time he's telling her that they're going to get her cleaned up. She's still whimpering about the blood that she's covered in.

I follow behind, wanting to give them their space, but also needing to see Sahara. These past few hours have made things so much clearer in my mind. It's time for me to make things right.

⚓

Edie assures me that Sahara won't wake up if I have a shower and offers to sit with her, so she isn't alone if she does. From the look she gives me I guess I look less than savory as well.

The hot water eases the ache in my shoulders and releases some of the tension that has been knotted up in there for days. I feel so much better for getting cleaned up, and dress quickly in jeans and a cotton shirt, the first clean clothes I come across.

Sahara is still asleep, as promised, when I return to her room. Edie rises from the chair in the corner of the room where she's been keeping watch, hugging me on her way past. "She'll be fine, " she assures me, "just please don't hurt her again."

Edie's words sting, but she's right. I've hurt Sahara with my actions. I need to put that right.

Ignoring the chair, I crawl onto the bed beside her, drawing her into my arms. This feels right, and for some reason the thought of the two of us together feels right as well. I just hope that when she wakes up, she'll give me a chance to prove that to her.

It's almost dark before she stirs beside me, looking around her in confusion as she tries to work out where she is. Sedation has a habit of leaving a drugged hangover feeling on waking, it always takes a few moments for your bearings to kick in.

"Holly!" she gasps, sitting up, alarm written all over her face.

"She's fine," I reassure her, "Declan's with her, she's going to be alright."

"But, the blood, there was so much blood," she grimaces.

"It wasn't Holly's," I quickly bring her up to date with what happened, and how Holly had escaped. Her body sags in relief against mine. I pull her closer, stroking her hair and reassuring her that it's all going to be okay now. She's safe, Holly's safe.

"What happens now?" she asks hesitantly.

"That depends on whether you're prepared to give me a second chance?" I ask her, watching her face to see if I can gauge her response.

"I though you didn't want me?" she sounds so forlorn that I feel like a total shit.

"What happened today made everything clear to me," I tell her. "I just kept thinking if that had been you, I don't think I could have survived losing you." She looks at me, I can see she doesn't quite believe me, I need to earn her trust back.

"Sahara, you're safe now, and it's up to you how you want to spend your future, you don't need to look over your shoulder any more. I'll totally understand if you decide to go it alone, but I'm sorry, I was a dick, I want you to choose us, to give me a chance to love you and care for you and keep you from harm."

I can't tell what she's thinking, and she's not saying anything. The moment drags out for what feels like an eternity.

"I'd like to see where it goes for us," she finally responds and it's like a lead weight is lifted from me.

"Thank fuck!" I exclaim. I can't help it, I pepper her face with kisses until she laughs and pushes me back.

"This might not work," her voice is serious, "I'm damaged Cam, I'm not good enough..."

"Stop right there," I interrupt her. "You are good enough, that's always been the problem, you're too good for me." I hold her face in my hands, looking her in the eye so she can see how sincere I am. "But, I'm going to be selfish now, I know you can do better than me, you deserve more, but I want you, I want us, if you'll give me a chance."

Sahara nods her head in agreement and I feel like the luckiest guy on the planet right now.

We kiss some more, and it's not long before I have her clothes off. Sahara huffs with impatience when she tries to undress me. "Do you always have to wear a belt!" she exclaims. I silence her with a kiss, and this time we don't fuck, we make sweet gentle love all night long.

40

Cam

There's an odd mood around the breakfast table the next morning, it's hard to put my finger on it. I think there's still an aura of fear surrounding the girls. As much as Declan and I are eager to deal with Jerry, he can wait. Right now, the girls are our priority.

Holly greeted us with a warm smile and a knowing wink when we entered the kitchen arm in arm. Sahara blushed before rushing over and engulfing her friend in a hug so tight I thought she'd never let go.

'So, what happens now?" Holly finally voices the question that everyone is thinking.

"We all live happily ever after," Declan jokingly responds. Holly gives him a withering look and the smile quickly falls from his face. "What do you want to happen?" he throws back at her.

Holly cocks her head on one side, considering her response. "I want to go back to Severed, but I'm guessing you want to stay here." She looks sad. Declan looks surprised.

"I never thought about staying here if I'm honest," he looks around the kitchen. "It won't be the same without her here, too many memories."

"Will you sell?" I ask him, an idea suddenly opening up in my mind.

"I don't know, I've not just got myself to think about, there's Fred and Edie and the rest of the farmhands. I need to do what's right for them." I can see that he's torn.

"I have an idea," I offer. "Why don't I stay here and manage the farm for you? I know Fred was wanting to cut back a bit and spend more time with Edie, and Sahara loves it here." She turns to me, the expression on her face one of hope and delight.

"That's not a bad idea," Declan considers it carefully. "Are you sure you won't miss city life?" He knows what a playboy I've been in the past.

Looking at Sahara, and the sheer joy she's radiating I know I'm making the right decision. I'm giving us the best chance at happiness I can think of, and if I'm honest with myself this place feels like home to me now.

"Of course, it depends on the remuneration package," I cock a smirk at Declan and watch as his face splits with laughter.

"Well, that all depends on your experience," he retorts, "not sure you have the expertise just yet to be making demands like that." Laughter breaks out around the table. The salary is the least of my concerns and he knows it, I know he'll be fair with me and in return I'll work my ass off for him. I finally want to stop wandering and set down roots, and this is the perfect place to do it.

Throughout the day we toss ideas around, and firm everything up as we picnic by the lake with the girls in the late afternoon sun. It's just what they needed. Holly seems to be coping as well as could be expected after her ordeal, yet I see nightmares ahead for her. I make a note to give her the counsellors phone number, as well as Declan.

Holly called us her Wounded Heroes, but now she's one of us. She showed so much sass and bravery yesterday. Both of our girls have endured so much, yet they're survivors just like us.

Nothing is said about Jerry during the day, other than reassuring Holly and Sahara that he's been dealt with and won't be bothering them again. They don't need to know what we have planned for him, or they'd have even worse nightmares.

It's nightfall and the girls are both asleep before we head out from the house to deal with him.

Jacko, Luke and Ryan have taken turns during the day guarding him and leave us to it when we finally arrive at the shed. We're dressed head to toe in black fatigues, faces daubed with camouflage paint. It's not like he doesn't know who we are, but we want to present as intimidating a presence as we can. He's been left alone whilst he's been here, no conversation, no food, no water, just silently watched by the dark guards in the shadows in front of him.

Jerry's strapped to a table, face down and naked as we'd requested. The fat white rolls of flesh on his back reflecting the weak light from the overhead lamp. He lifts his weary head and glares at us as we approach.

"Do you know who you're dealing with?" he asks with mock bravado. "Do you have any idea who my Uncle is and what he'll do to you?" he threatens.

"Yep," I pop out the word. "Jack Snr gave me his blessing. He can't stand filthy perverts like you who trade in little girls." I take great pleasure at the way his face blanches as the understanding hits, he has no way of escaping his fate and no one will be coming to look for him.

"I'd get comfortable if I were you," Declan suggests to him, "It's going to be a very long night." Jerry pales a little more as he sees the flash of light reflecting from the knife blade in Declan's hand.

Over the course of the next six hours Jerry answers everything we ask, turns out he has no tolerance for pain at all. After the first blade sliced into his back he couldn't wait to rat out his contacts. Every time he hesitates with an answer, another cut appears in the fleshy rolls on his back. Blood drips slowly from the wounds onto the tarpaulin sheet below the table. Not enough to cause any permanent damage, but the steady drip onto the plastic below ensures Jerry's attention stays on us.

I take careful notes as Jerry reveals the trafficking network he has used to buy and sell, some of the buyer's names I recognize and am shocked by. They're prominent figures in society, and I'm appalled by the sick depravity Jerry reveals. This intel will all be anonymously handed over to the authorities when we've finished.

Jerry was naive if he thought by telling us what we wanted

to know that we'd let him go. It was never an option, we'd made a promise to Jack Snr that we'd uphold. He's going to disappear once and for all. After kidnaping Holly his fate was more than sealed, we could have made it quick and painless for him at the end but going after one of ours made that option obsolete. We'd never given him cause to think there was a way out of this for him. We'd discussed various ways of putting him out of his misery, but it was Luke who'd come up with the solution for us, he's the quiet one of us for a reason, he's seen some really dark shit and I admit I cringed when he came up with his suggestion. It's a scenario he'd walked in on in Afghanistan when they'd been too late to rescue a child molester. There's a certain dark irony to making this Jerry's fate, but I still think it's as twisted as fuck. The fat slob deserves no sympathy and no mercy though, he's brought this all on himself with his choice of career. We'll spare Jack Snr a lot of the details of the trade his nephew participated in, and certainly the way he's going to meet his end. All he needs to know is the matter has been dealt with and Jerry won't be darkening his name or his door any more.

When we're confident that Jerry has no more intel for us, we bid him farewell, showing him the lethally sharp long blade that is going to end his miserable life. It's not going to be a quick end, but we're not staying to keep him company. He deserves a solitary death, full of pain and fear. It's the least we can do for the victims who didn't survive his machinations.

Standing behind him I take the blade from Declan, he doesn't need to do this, he already has enough nightmares without adding to them. Jerry's pleas and screams fall on deaf ears as I take the blade and insert it up his ass, twisting as I go to inflict the most possible damage to his internal organs. He can scream as loudly as he wants, no one is around to hear it.

"Maybe we should consider getting some pigs," I quip as we leave the shed, Jerry's body bleeding out slowly behind us. "It would certainly help to hide the bodies around here." It's gallows humor, but I don't want to think about how painfully slow Jerry's demise is going to be.

"Let's get back to our girls," Declan suggests. "I need to wash the stench of him from me."

Using Declan's favorite phrase, I respond positively. "It would be rude not to!"

EPILOGUE

Some months later...

Sahara

$\mathcal{I}$'m not sure what's wrong with Cam but he's bouncing around like a toddler full of e numbers and sugar this morning. I'm really not in the mood for it, if I'm honest I'd rather just spend the next twenty-four hours in bed, hiding under the covers and trying not to think about what today is.

Come to think of it everyone is a bit hyper round here this week, maybe I'm just being overly sensitive. Declan and Holly are coming to stay for a few days this afternoon, perhaps that's what's got everyone in such a tizzy.

"Don't stay in bed too long, Sugar," Cam kisses me before he leaves the room, I swear he's on something. He does know what today means to me because I told him but judging from the way he's behaving he's forgotten. Typical man. I sigh and sink back into the pillows, determined to allow myself a little time to wallow in my own pity. I deserve it after all.

My heart is physically aching today. I glance over at the sun streaming through the net curtain and curse it for its cheerfulness. Today should be stormy and rainy and full of thunder and lightning to match the hurt within my soul.

Sophia turns four today, my little blonde-haired angel that my arms ache so desperately for. Cam has made me so happy these past few months, but that's the one thing in my life he can't fix bless him. We've talked about children, in a few years perhaps, but he's never had a child. I can't expect him to know the heartbreak I feel every day. Having another child won't fix that, nothing can.

Life on the farm is what I needed, I love the countryside, the way of life, and Fred and Edie have taken me under their wing. They're practically the grandparents I never had. Fred's looking much happier now he's cut back on his working hours, but he takes a lot of pleasure from showing Cam the ropes.

It's never going to be the same for the others without Gran here, but thanks to Declan agreeing to Cam running the farm for him, they've managed to stay together. I hadn't realized before I came here just how much of a micro community this place is. Everyone looks out for each other, and everyone seems to genuinely care.

I've found a kind of peace here, and I feel more comfortable here than anywhere else. There's just that one thing missing.

The noise below isn't conducive to a day full of pity fest, so I decide I may as well get up after all. I can't allow myself to drown in my sorrows every birthday and Christmas. I did the best thing for Sophia and that's an end of it.

It's not until I'm under the shower that I allow the tears to fall, thankfully no one can hear me sob my heart out in here, and if my eyes are a little red then I'll just say I got shampoo in them. I'm a little pissed that Cam hasn't remembered what today is, and that sets off a fresh jag of crying.

It's a glorious day so I dress in jean shorts and a crop vest, there's nothing on the calendar today so I'm hoping I can maybe go for a walk by the lake and sit there and reflect. It's my favorite place on the farm.

Edie is in the kitchen when I get down and passes me a coffee that I take to the kitchen table. I'm not sure what she's doing in the main house, Cam kept the housekeeper on after Gran passed, but there's no sign of her and Edie's bustling away with something on the counter and grinning like a loon whilst she sings along to the radio.

Seriously, what have they put in the water around here lately and why haven't I had any?

Cam breezes into the kitchen and I have to admire the view in front of me. Some days I feel like I need to pinch myself, I can't believe that this man is mine. We came so close to making a mess of things, I'm so glad he thought I was worth fighting for.

"Right, get your pretty ass up, we're going for a picnic," he grins at me as he reaches for the picnic blanket I had missed on the counter.

"But... I haven't had breakfast yet!" I whine, "and I haven't made a picnic either."

"Ahh, but I have." Edie comes over with a basket covered in a gingham cloth and hands it to Cam. A look passes between them that I can't identify, and she gives him a hug. What the hell is going on here today and have I woken up in an alternate universe?

"Come on sleepy head, it's not my fault you wouldn't get up this morning." Cam calls over his shoulder as he heads out the door. I want to swear at him for forgetting what today is, but I won't, not in front of Edie. Once we're out of hearing though that's a different matter.

Cam is striding ahead of me and I hurry to catch up, so I can tell him what I think, but the look on his face gives me pause. He looks so happy I don't have the heart to tell him how much he's hurt me with his forgetfulness today of all days.

He carries everything in his left hand, reaching for me with his right. I take his offered hand and we walk side by side, enjoying the peace as I realize we are heading to the lake. I guess he's not as forgetful as I thought, he knows this is my quiet place.

When we reach the lake, he places the blanket on the ground for us and we lay down side by side looking at the cloudless sky through the canopy of the trees. There's a quiet trickling sound from the water on the lake shore, it's such a relaxing spot.

Cam turns to look at me and somehow, he's not quite so bubbly as he was earlier. "Are you happy with me, Sahara?"

There's a hint of nervousness in his question. It's not like him to be quite so serious.

"Of course I am, Cam. I thought you knew that?"

He reaches over and slowly traces a finger down the side of my face, almost as though he's committing me to memory.

"I'm not good with words, Sahara, you know that," he's right, he's definitely a man of action rather than a man of words. "I know I fought us being together, but that was the stupidest thing I ever did." He sits up now and pulls me up into a sitting position beside him. "What I'm trying to say," he pauses, and my man looks nervous as heck right now, "well, what I'm trying to say is that you're the best thing that ever happened to me, and, well, Sahara, would you marry me?" he rushes the last words out as he fumbles in his pocket at the same time. When he's finished speaking he shows me a blue velvet box, opening it to reveal a small but perfect antique diamond engagement ring.

I'm lost for words. I just sit there gawping at the ring, my mouth opening and closing like a fish.

"Well?" he looks at me, he's started to go a little pale now anticipating a negative response.

"Oh my God, oh yes, yes, yes!" I screech out as I finally find my voice, throwing my arms around his neck.

Cam lifts the ring from the box placing it on my hand, it's a little loose but there's no way I'm taking it off. I hold my hand out in front of me, twisting it one way and another as I watch the sun sparkling off the diamond.

"Is this why you were all so giddy the last couple of days?" I laugh whilst still admiring my ring.

"Might have been," he confesses. "Fred and Edie knew what I had planned."

"Come here," putting my hand behind his head I draw his face closer to mine and kiss him. The kiss deepens, and picnic ignored, we celebrate our engagement on the picnic blanket by the lake.

It's early afternoon before we pack up and start to head back to the house. Cam has been clock watching for the last half hour and I can't stand it anymore. I hadn't realized he was quite so keen to see Declan again.

I'm so glad that Declan and Holly are coming now, they can help us celebrate. As we near the farmhouse I can see them on the porch waiting for us, along with Fred and Edie. At our approach they all rise and look towards us expectantly.

I wave my hand in greeting, the sun catching the diamond and sparkling away. There's a loud cheer in response. As we reach the porch I'm engulfed in hugs and kisses of congratulation. I'm so grateful for my new family right now.

Fred comes out of the house with a bottle of chilled champagne and a tray of flutes. Cam pops the cork and the spray of the bubbly catches me. I can't help laughing.

I turn as I hear the sound of a car coming down the lane. I wasn't expecting any other visitors today and turn to ask Cam who it is. He's not looking at me. His eyes are focused on the approaching vehicle. A sick feeling hits my stomach, I know Cam has told me that Jerry has been dealt with, but what if its him, or one of his cronies?

Cam's been off on a few trips he won't tell me about, and I'm scared that he's still handling the repercussions from the warehouse, that the nightmare isn't over. The car has come to a stop now in front of the porch and Cam is moving towards it. I step back a little, but Holly puts a reassuring hand on my arm and eases me closer to the front of the porch.

The driver's door opens, and I almost collapse when my father steps from the car, then my mother appears on the other side. Cam goes to greet my father and its obvious they've met before. I can't move as my mother heads to the back of the car, hope rising, along with fear.

The rear passenger door opens and my mother leans in, fiddling with something. When she stands she's holding my angel in her arms. She's grown so much I almost don't recognize her. It's been over a year since I last held my baby. I nearly trip as I run down the steps to my mother, stopping in front of her, my arms aching to reach out but not daring to.

My mother senses my hesitation and holds Sophia out towards me. I grab her greedily, snatching her to my chest, my nose in her hair breathing in that baby scent that I've missed so much. It feels like an eternity but can only have been moments before Sophia starts wriggling in my grasp, I'm holding her too tight.

I loosen my grip, still not letting her go. "It's my birfday." She grins up at me. "I's four."

"I know baby girl, I know. Happy Birthday, Angel." I smile back at her.

"I's not Angel," she giggles, "I's Soffeea"

I look at Cam who's watching me with such love in his heart I could burst. Could today get any better?

My father walks over to my mother and they stand there facing me. I'm not sure what to say, I don't want to let Sophia go or this moment to end, although I know it will have to.

"I'm sorry," my father actually apologizes to me. "I'm so sorry for what we did to you." My father is actually crying in front of me. I've never seen my father cry. He pulls me and Sophia into a hug and my mother joins in. I've no idea what the hell is happening here, but I'm even more convinced I woke up in an alternate universe this morning.

"This young man came to see me, told me what a jerk I'd been and how my actions almost got you killed." My father can't stop hugging me, much the same way I'm holding tightly to Sophia. "I'm so sorry." He kisses my forehead, he hasn't done that since I was Sophia's age. "He asked me for my permission to marry you, and he told me I had to give you your baby back. He was right, I'm so sorry."

I look around me in shock, Cam, Fred and Declan are grinning like loons and Edie and Holly are dabbing at their eyes with tissues. Is this really happening?

My father clears his throat, wiping away a tear as he does so. "Now I understand we have a birthday party to get to for this little girl." Sophia cheers and wriggles to be put down, running into the house. As I follow I find the whole downstairs has been decorated for a four-year old's birthday party and there are piles of presents in the corner. Cam comes up behind me, wrapping his arms around me.

"Sorry I kept it a secret from you," he whispers in my ear.

"I forgive you," I reply as I take in the scene in front of me.

I'm still the little girl who wants to believe in a fairy tale ending, and that I'm the best thing that ever happened to someone.

Family. Love. Home.

Guess some fairytales do come true after all.

EXTRACT FROM DECLAN

Declan (Wounded Heroes #1)

DECLAN PROLOGUE

Declan

$\mathcal{T}$he touch of my fingers sends a small tremor through her. I try to keep the massage firm, yet tender. I can already see some of the tension leaving her body. She groans as I knead the hard knot at the base of her neck. This past week has been a living nightmare for all of us, but especially her and the stress has really knotted her neck and shoulders.

My hands leave her skin for a moment as I reach for more body lotion. She moans in protest. There's a delicate hint of coconut in the air as I warm it in my hands before applying it at the base of her spine.

I knead up and down her back, leaving a trail of warmth where I've passed. I can feel my cock twitching in my tight boxer briefs, begging to be let loose. It's been too long since I allowed myself that particular pleasure. After everything that's happened I wasn't sure it would show interest in sex again, I'm pleased that it is, but I can't. Not here. Not now.

Georgia is laying face down underneath me, dressed only in skimpy briefs so that I can massage her back. My legs are astride hers and I'm pretty sure she can feel my cock pushing against her. She says nothing though.

How the fuck did I find myself here? On this bed and in this position? This is my friend's widow for fucks sake. I need to show him some respect. I need to remember the man that he was, not the shell he had become. He sank so low that there was no coming back. That's why I'm here. We buried him today, so the last place I should be right now is in his widow's bed.

I couldn't ignore Georgia's scream though as she'd woken from a nightmare, or the fat tears rolling down her face. She's too young to be a widow; she's not even forty. She has her whole life ahead of her. I'd consoled her by drawing her into my arms, sitting on the edge of the bed and pulling her close. She'd whimpered when my hand touched her back. The downside of living with Max for these past few months had been the abuse. She may have outgrown most of the bruises but the residual pain was still there.

I'd offered her a back rub in my innocence, and that's how I came to find myself here now, sitting on top of her and desperately begging my cock to go back into its usual state of stupor.

There's something sensuous about caressing a woman's skin, and it's turning me on. As awful as it sounds it helps that I can't see Georgia's face. I couldn't do this if I looked her in the eye. I need to just pretend she's some anonymous stranger if I've any chance of getting through the rest of this night.

Georgia moans as I release a particularly deep knot in her shoulder, but it sounds more like a moan of passion than relief.

"Declan," she pleads. "I need you. I need this." She whimpers.

"I can't." I whisper back. "I can't do it to Max." I apologize.

"Fuck Max." She hisses. "He didn't give a shit about either of us these past few months. I need this." She pauses. "And from the feel of your cock digging into my ass you need it too." She reasons.

She's right. I do need it. But I can't.

"I can't look you in the eye." I apologize.

"Then don't." She reasons. She reaches down behind her, pulling her almost non-existent underwear down and raising her ass slightly. I can see her glistening pussy. She's wet for me and I know for sure that my cock is hard for her.

I dismiss the guilt from my mind and release myself from my boxer shorts. Without allowing myself time to think about it I push into her. Fuck! That feels so good. It feels so tight and deep. I pause for a moment just enjoying the sensation, and Georgia lets out a loud groan of satisfaction.

"That feels fucking amazing." She almost purrs.

Slowly I move in and out of her, each time it feels like I've gone deeper than the last. Her legs are trapped together between mine by her shoved down underwear and her ass is gripping tightly to my cock as I move in and out.

She moves a hand to caress my leg. I stop her by holding her arms down. From the satisfied moans she's making, it's clear she likes that. Her face is almost hidden in the mattress, the pillow already tossed aside. She's got short hair, I want to grab hold of it and pull her head back each time I push into her, but it's too short for that. It's just long enough to hide her face, and that's probably a good thing. If I saw her face right now I suspect my cock would deflate faster than a popped balloon.

The only sounds in the room are the slap of flesh against flesh as my movements become stronger as do our mutual groans of pleasure. I slap her ass sharply, and when she doesn't protest I do it again. She's pushing her ass back up against me, silently begging for more. I give it to her.

That's when it all goes to shit. I'm having the best sex I've had in months, fuck it I'm having the only sex I've had in months, when I hear it.

A car backfires outside and I lose it. Suddenly I'm not in this suburban bedroom; I'm back in Afghanistan the day it happened. I can feel the heat, taste the sand in my mouth, and hear the screams of the other guys.

I snap out of it, just in time. My hands are round Georgia's neck and I'm strangling her. She can barely breathe, let alone make a sound and her face is going a shade of purple. I release my hands quickly.

Georgia draws in a deep gulping breath of air before collapsing back down to the mattress and taking shallow breaths.

"What the fuck!" She croaks, her voice barely there and raspy.

What do I say; how the fuck do I explain the nightmare that I live constantly? I can't. Instead I do the most dick move possible. I pull out of her and rush from the room without explanation.

Within minutes my bag is packed and I'm gone. Driving to an unknown destination in the dark of the night. I didn't even say I was sorry.

I 'm not sure where to go so I just drive. I'm not fit to be around normal people. Something broke in me out in Afghanistan, and I'm not sure I can ever be mended.

So I drive, and wait to see where the road takes me.

ACKNOWLEDGMENTS

A book like this doesn't happen without a support network, the size of which you wouldn't believe. I can only count my blessings when it comes to my amazing #bookfamily who have supported me and encouraged me over the last few years.

The biggest thanks as always has to go to the readers, without you, there wouldn't be a Cam. You are the reason I write.

My book besties, authors K L Shandwick and Tracie Podger have been there for me every step of the way and have also been known to verbally kick me back into writing when I was starting to doubt I could do it.

Author T L Wainright, Fiona Wilson, Nadia Debowska-Stepehens, Naomi Connor, and Francessca Wingfield guided me in the right direction when I missed out speech marks, got names confused and left gaps in the plot. Thank you ladies for putting up with me, especially when I only shared a few chapters at a time and made you cry.

To my crazy number one stalker Margaret Hassebrock and number two stalker Beckie Hughes, you don't know how much it means to have readers who love me like you guys do and meeting you at signings has been an amazing experience.

To Yvonne Eason, Chele McKenzie, Lesley Edwards and Colette Goodchild, who have been there for me through some hard times and sad memories, thank you.

And to everyone else who I should have named and probably forgot, thank you!

#bookfamily

ABOUT THE AUTHOR

About Ava Manello

Ava is a passionate reader, blogger, publisher, and author who loves nothing more than helping other Indie authors publish their books be that reviewing, beta reading, formatting or proofreading. She will always be a reader first and foremost.

She loves erotic suspense that's well written and engages the reader, and loves promoting the heck out of it for her favourite authors.

As Ava says: "I took a chance and followed a dream when I wrote my first book. It was scary, challenging and hard work, but above all it was worth it."

STALK AVA MANELLO

Amazon Author Page
http://geni.us/AvaM

Ava Manello Reader Group (Facebook)
https://www.facebook.com/groups/613212832386624/

Ava Manello Facebook Page
http://www.facebook.com/AvaManello

Ava Manello Website
http://www.avamanello.co.uk

Ava Manello Twitter
http://www.twitter.com/AvaManello

Ava Manello Instagram
https://www.instagram.com/avamanello/

Ava Manello BookBub
https://www.bookbub.com/authors/ava-manello

Ava Manello Newsletter
http://eepurl.com/bOJXE9

ALSO BY AVA MANELLO

Declan (Wounded Heroes #1)

Amazon: http://geni.us/Declan

Other Channels: https://books2read.com/u/bOaqYg

Severed Angel (Severed MC #1)

Amazon: http://geni.us/SAFREE

Other Channels: https://www.books2read.com/b/bxg5k4

Carnal Desire (Severed MC #2)

Amazon: http://geni.us/CarnalDesire

Other Channels: https://www.books2read.com/b/4j1nDm

Severed Justice (Severed MC #3)

Amazon: http://geni.us/severedjustice

Other Channels: https://www.books2read.com/b/bWrlz4

Carnal Persuasion (Severed MC #4)

Amazon: http://geni.us/CarnalPersuasion

Other Channels: https://www.books2read.com/b/baBG23

Strip Back (Naked Nights #1)

Amazon: http://geni.us/StripBack

Other Channels: https://books2read.com/u/bzyaL4

Strip Teaser (Naked Nights #0.5)

Amazon: http://geni.us/StripTeaser

Other Channels: https://books2read.com/u/47XEab

The Non Adventures of Alice the Erotic Author

Amazon: http://geni.us/AliceNonAdventures

Other Channels: https://books2read.com/u/bzPvVq

28897681R00163

Printed in Poland
by Amazon Fulfillment
Poland Sp. z o.o., Wrocław